Maria R. Springer
Maja's Kitchen LLC
12300 Rosslare Ridge Rd #403
Timonium, MD 21093

Also By Victor Merkel

Fiction

Misery Mountain

Biography

Constant Reminder

Cover design by:

Miles Abernethy Design

480-231-1118

info@milesabernethy.com

TAILGUNNER

TAILGUNNER

WAR DEFINES US...IF WE LET IT

VICTOR MERKEL

ANN FROMMER

Dedicated to my brother, Walter (Buck) Merkel, Jr., who answered Uncle Sam's call to defend our country as a B-17 tailgunner. Also to his daughter Leslie Merkel Kruize.

Introduction

This story rests somewhere between fact and fiction. Buck Merkel existed. He lived with his parents and three younger brothers in New England Valley, a small rural community outside of Tamaqua, Pennsylvania.

The family and their day to day lives followed a path close to this fictional rendering. However, Buck's capture and prisoner of war aftermath are pure imagination, created by intensive research.

As for Ilona László her character is also fictitious, using a combination of two strong women, Ann Frommer detailed this heroine's courageous escape from East Europe based on someone who succeeded in eluding the Nazis.

Acknowledgements - Victor Merkel

This story remained buried in history until my brother, Buck, passed in the winter of 2011. With Ann Frommer's help, his legacy will be preserved.

Much gratitude to my wife, Fran. In spite of overwhelming obstacles she supported me throughout the writing of this novel.

also

Deb Merkel Wanamaker, my daughter, and her family, for encouraging words.

Taylor, Kaylin, Colton, Aiden, Sammi and Ella for their unconditional love.

Ernie Feavel and the entire clan, for listening to my rambling early drafts of *Tailgunner*.

Leroy and Mary Bridygham, personal friends of Buck during the war years.

Bob Knaepoli, division manager of a major electronics' manufacturer, who taught me how to swim with the sharks.

Randy Rizzo, airline pilot and instructor, who guided me through Private Pilot training near Chicago, IL. Through his eyes, I gained an understanding of the fragile dynamics a B-17 had to maintain in keeping aloft.

- Vijaya Schartz, Phoenix, AZ, mentor and award
- winning author, who helped me to understand
- the world of publishing and marketing.
-
- Troubador's writing club members, Carla,
- Bob, Linda, and Ray, who illuminated my
- path to professional level writing, story-
- telling and novel lay-out.
-
- In loving memory of my family, Walter, Sr.,
- Bernice, Miles and Paul, who belong to the
- ages now. They lived imperfect lives, yet
- possessed a strong will to rise above the
- throbbing wail of humanity.

Acknowledgements - Ann Frommer

A life-long dream of writing my first novel was realized after former schoolmate Vic Merkel & I reconnected after many years.

For Robi, my husband - who introduced me to Budapest and his mother country, Hungary. Here, we spend many of our happiest times.

also

- Greg Gordon, my son who has a passion for history and gave me the excuse to read him history books as a child.
- My kids, Geoffery Scott & Tina Gordon.
- Claude Hagelberg, my friend and WWII history consult.
- Todd Tyminsky, DC, my chiropractor who introduced me to his former classmate Zsolt Kálbori, DC, in Budapest Zsolt kept my back pain free allowing me to remain for long periods of time in Budapest.
- Major Mark Morgan, history teacher and WWII authority at Carson Long Academy in New Bloomfield, PA.
- Deborah Fennelly, my friend and proof reader.
- Rosemary Cooke, my next door neighbor and writing coach.
- Tomas Tuschak, who lived through some of these times and gave insight into Ilona's life.
- Maria Tumas, my cousin whose year living in London gave me many good tips.
- My Arner cousins: Sylvia, Arner Herman who tipped me off about my co-author's first book, "Misery Mountain"; Mickey Arner and his son Billy, professional pilots, who filled in information on my former pilot father, Edgar Arner and his brother, Stanley and their barnstorming antics.

- Dr. Jack Brous, my "special effects" expert.
- Diane Panzer, a friend and author, who encouraged me to write.
- Members of the "Breakfast Babes" who listened patiently to my chapter readings and gave me insight and advice.
- Jean Steveley, a war bride who gave me personal insight to her life in London.
- Dr. Robert W. Butts, Artistic Director of the Baroque Orchestra of NJ.
- The Library of the Chathams whose shelves I combed for great references.
- Darren O'Neill from the Music Department of the Morris County, NJ. Library.
- Judy Banks, M.D. and Judith Sipos, M.D. my medical authorities.
- Stephen Henden, my London contact and V1 & V2 expert.
- Special tribute to the memory of my father, Edgar (Hop) Arner who never tired of telling his flying stories. He truly was the daring and dashing pilot that wore the white scarf and leather flight jacket.

Apologies to Arner's Airport in Lehighton, PA. Its existence provided good story material but is owned by another Arner.

CONTENTS

Chapter 1

Gunnery School

"What the hell? Keep still for 2 seconds, you son of a bitch." I gripped the spade handles even tighter, swinging the turret to the left, my gun sight chasing after the god damn barrel-shaped target, as it flapped behind a tow plane.

My pilot pulled out of his dive just as I clenched thumbs full down on the butterfly trigger, the whole frame of the turret, jerking back and forth in quick short bursts. Empty 50 cal brass flew everywhere, adding to all the other distractions.

Our fighter leveled off, finishing a good day's training. I smiled, knowing that out of two hundred rounds at least twenty five percent found their target. Our aircraft landed in the mild Las Vegas weather and taxied to the tarmac.

Before we could stow our gear, a loud buzzer, rasped throughout the training facility. Our training sergeant bellowed, "Attention. Attention. Lock your artillery and meet at the ready room."

About thirty of us filed into the large area, filled with chairs, a podium and map of Europe on the back wall. A contingent of officers stood at one side of the platform.

The sergeant took long strides to the front and announced, "All right, all right. You know this day has been coming for a long time. This phase of your training is almost over. Before you move on, Major Bennett has some important information. So listen up."

"Good afternoon gentlemen. So far, you've survived preflight school, navigator school and gunnery school, quite an accomplishment for a crew that's barely mastered the art of shaving."

I laughed along with the rest of the team. It felt good to take a whimsical look at myself. After all, just over a year ago, I was a senior at Tamaqua High, one of Pennsylvania's coal-town schools.

"But seriously…you've done us proud, each and every one of you. Soon, you'll put this training to use, fighting the Nazis."

*****

His words faded into background noise as I remembered how it all started. When I reached fourteen, Pop took me hunting a few days before Thanksgiving. At sunrise, he positioned the 12 gauge on my shoulder and taught me how to aim the sight.

"Remember, when you see a deer, take a deep breath, aim

for the chest and squeeze the trigger nice and slow." Well, I never had the pleasure of putting one of those long legged critters in the line of fire, at least not for most of the morning. In fact, we had started to head back to the car.

We just cleared the woods when a stag with huge antlers crossed our path. Pop and I stopped in our tracks. Before my father could say a word, I raised the barrel of my shotgun and fired both barrels.

The buck dropped like a sack of bricks, never moving, while Pop looked on in shock. My heart raced with excitement and I knew forever more - one of my talents lay in the ability to wield a firearm with deadly accuracy.

*****

And how could I forget the aviator and neighbor who also prepared me for this day, during the summer of 1939. At sixteen, I worked as a bricklayer's helper for Pop. In July, my father and I tackled a project for Arner's Airport in Lehighton.

On the drive to Arner's for the first day of work, I inquired, "Pop, what kind of structure does the airport want to build?"

"Well, according to the owner, Edgar Arner, he needs an observation tower on the south side of the airstrip. I never built one before but from the plans, it's like a small two story building except with a lot of windows on top. Maybe you know Mr. Arner, he and his family live just down the road from us."

"Here in New England Valley?"

"Yeah, across from the chicken farmer."

"Hmmm, seems to me I heard about him and his brother Stanley's barnstorming antics last year."

"No doubt, Buck. It was the most excitement this area saw in quite a while."

Pop and I arrived at the flat, grassy field by day-break. We parked near the surrounding trees, as far away from the runway as possible. Numerous airplanes lined the sides of the strip. I didn't recognize most of them except for the World War One Jennys.

A twin engine aircraft fired up its engines, creating a deep growling rumble of sound accompanied by a solid blast of air. It taxied to the far end of the strip and lined up with the runway. For several seconds it just sat there and within a blink the roar of unbridled power catapulted the craft skyward.

I stood next to Pop, just feet from the runway, my eyes following the plane as it disappeared from sight. The sheer magic of its flight left me astounded.

"Good morning, Mr. Remke."

We turned around to find a tall man, sporting a dark brown leather jacket and long white scarf loosely draped around his neck.

Pop beamed as he responded, "Top of the morning to you,

Mr. Arner."

"Please, just call me Hop, short for Hopper." He pointed to his leg. "Unlike Curly Howard, I don't use comedy to hide my limp.

"Also, you'll find, on this airfield, we all share the same value - love of flying. No prima donnas here."

"Okay…Hop. You can call me Walter and this is my oldest boy, Walter Junior, but everybody calls him Buck."

"Good enough, from now on, it's Walter and Buck. I imagine you want to take a look at the foundation we poured several weeks ago."

"Yeah, if it's cured, we can start this morning."

With the background noise of airplanes taking off and landing, we marched to a wood frame, single story building near the access road. A sign out front read - OPERATIONS. Next to it sat the slab with wood forms, not yet removed and a canvas top. Pop removed the covering and surveyed the 17 foot by 17 foot base.

Pop nodded, "Okay, no cracks or low spots. I'll take one last check with my level but we will lay several courses today. And thanks for unloading the cinder blocks close by. Not so much for me, but Buck will appreciate it."

"I ordered five hundred to get you started, Walter. Lehighton Brick Works can deliver in 1 day so just let me know how many you need.

"As for you, young man - looks like you have the hardest part of this job. Do you plan to enter the trade like your father?"

"Maybe. Pop and I talked about it, but with two years of high school left...anything can happen before graduation."

"Good for you. Old Man Death takes us fast enough, so sample what life has to offer before you set a course."

"Walter – I have business that needs tending. If you need me, I'll be in the Operations Building."

"We have everything under control here, Hop. I'll check in with you later."

I retrieved tools from the car while Pop strung a plumb line for the first course. Soon after, I mixed cement and laid cinder blocks on the ground, around the base. Pop started to trowel cement on the slab and lay each block, one by one, in perfect alignment. We worked through the sweltering July heat until mid-afternoon when Pop completed the third course.

"We'll end it here, for now, Buck. You can cart the tools back to the car and meet me at the Operations Building."

Loading trowels, levels, brick hammers, etc., into the trunk, I hot-footed it to join Pop. Upon entry, it seemed a different world. Aeronautical maps plus aircraft pictures covered the walls, and squawking, from what looked like a radio set, filled the room. I heard a pilot requesting temperature, wind direction and landing information. Hop keyed a microphone and responded to the pilots' questions. A fan in the corner moved the otherwise hot air.

A large desk covered with neat stacks of paperwork occupied the middle of the room plus an ensemble of table and four chairs sat off to one side.

Pop appeared tired as he relaxed in one of the captain's chairs, a cigarette in his left hand, bottle of soda in the other. Hop sat across from him, nervously tapping the base of his microphone while sipping a Coke. Thick beads of moisture trickled down the sides of his bottle onto a coaster.

"I just informed Hop, our first day went well. We should wrap this up in the next two or three weeks."

Hop chimed in, "It is great news. Looks like the control tower will be up and running before Labor Day. Buck, can I offer you a soda? I know it's been a long day."

"Sure. By the way, I have a question. Why do you need a tower?"

Handing me a Coke from his fridge, he responded, "One reason. Surplus war planes have flooded the market. The number of pilots has mushroomed in the last twenty years. I need visual confirmation of aircraft during peak periods of activity. There have been some bewildering accidents across the United States simply because of too much congestion."

"Mr....uh...Hop, with all those pilots out there, could someone like me afford flying lessons?"

"Someone like you? Buck – young people, like you, will shape the future of aviation. But money is irrelevant if you don't have the desire."

"For sure, I feel a certain amount of curiosity. If we can work something out, I'd like to start some training, on weekends, and see where it goes.

"Sorry Pop, for getting ahead of myself. What do you think about me learning to fly, as a pastime?"

"You know your own mind. When I reached your age, I took a fancy to racing horses for the zillionaires out of Philly on Saturday afternoons. It only lasted for two summers but I relished the excitement. Your mother might have something to say but I think she'll come around."

Hop reached into what looked like a King Edward cigar box and pulled out a stogie. Striking a wooden match, he ignited the end and puffed until a sweet smelling vapor filled the room. For a few seconds, he seemed to savor the aroma of his smoke, and then lowered himself back into the chair, turning his attention to me.

"How does this sound, Buck? Come by the airport early Saturday morning. I'll give you an aerial tour of Lehighton. If you still want to go forward, then my brother Stanley will guide you through ground school on things like – how a plane stays aloft, weather, how to fly from Lehighton to…anywhere.

"Next, I'll only bill for gas used on the first hour and kick-in a flight lesson for free. Once a student commits to getting a

Private License, my brother Stanley and I have a pay-as-you-go plan. So...you can fly as many or few hours as you want."

"I'd like to take the air tour, Hop. Thanks for explaining how everything works."

"You're welcome, but thank me by helping your father finish the tower."

Pop shoved his weary looking frame to a standing position, "Hop, appreciate the cold libation. My boy and I will take our leave and head for home. We'll show up tomorrow, at sunrise, ready to work."

"I look forward to it, Walter."

We came back the next day and every day that followed for three and one half weeks. The first level had openings for two doors and several small windows. Carpenters installed stairs and a wood floor for the second level. Pop laid four courses on the top story in preparation for the glass contractor. When my father lay the last block, we all walked to the ground level and just stood there, looking up. Except for the glass and roof, the tower stood tall.

Hop smiled, nodding his approval and shook my father's hand. "You just made my dream a reality. Thank you."

"You're welcome. I have to confess, although I've built almost every type of building, this tower represents my most unique achievement. It can withstand the strongest wind and will be here long after we're gone."

As for me, I took the free tour over Lehighton with Hop and enjoyed soaring above the clutter of mankind below. For the next two weekends, I attended ground school, under Stanley's direction, which helped me understand the mystery of aviation.

After Pop finished the tower, every Saturday morning, I arrived at Arner's Airport, by seven. Hop's World War One Jenny, Number 74, always sat near the end of the runway, gassed and waiting. Hop taught me take-offs and landings, flying a course and emergency landings.

By August, with a mere 5 hours of flight time, Hop approved me for solo flight. At first I felt nervous until the plane left the runway. Then I felt free of the world and with the wind blowing against my goggles, I flew to places like Allentown, Harrisburg or Wilkes Barre. With my attention focused on keeping the craft airborne, I didn't think about the empty seat in front of me, until I landed.

The first signs of fall started with cooler mornings, changing color of leaves and high school. Hop began to train me on advanced maneuvers like stalling the Jenny – on purpose – so it started to fall out of the sky. Not a good feeling, but I needed to know its limitations. Also, we climbed to 10,000 feet and over-controlled the ailerons into a spin. Hop said the control-surfaces had factory design problems and at low altitude, almost always resulted in a crash.

Just before Halloween, I spent two hours on a training flight of Douglas' DC2. Hop rode the right seat to document the trip and enter it into my log book. The silver, 2 engine plane sent my stomach churning as I performed basic maneuvers - take off, cruise on a course due east for Newark Airport, land and return to Arner's Airport.

After I shut the DC2's system down, Hop asked me to join him in the office. Sitting on a hard wooden chair in front of his desk, I questioned, "Do we have any more training?"

Hop lit a King Edward cigar, leaned back in his leather bound office chair and smiled, "Buck, ninety days ago, I never anticipated your persistence and dedication. With well over ten hours of instruction, today's flight on the DC2 is your crowning achievement. You've proved your worth. I have nothing left to teach you…except from this day forward you'll face the world with more confidence. The ability to think a problem through and take action doesn't only apply to airplanes.

"Next Saturday, an FAA examiner will fly up from Philly and give you a check ride on the Jenny. Buck, you'll have a Private Pilot's License by November."

I stood up and exclaimed, "All right! Thanks for all your help and believing in me, Hop."

Hop walked to the front side of his desk and shook my hand. He also added, "I'll make sure the Tamaqua Courier prints an article on your achievement."

Tamaqua High School seemed all abuzz when Hop's editorial hit the streets. Over the following weeks, I came to understand, my view of the world had changed. I felt more self-assured and believed - whatever goal I set - will be achieved.

Although the frequency of my flying fell to only a few hours a month, Hop and I remained friends until the war took me away.

*****

I accepted these skills, hunting and aviation, as the random passions of a teenager. My last two years in high school seemed care free until the spring of 1942. The curse of war fell on everyone, including Tamaqua High seniors soon to graduate. When I enlisted, my preference seemed obvious - Army Air Force pilot or gunner.

However, I quickly came to understand, ripping out the roots of my peaceful life in New England Valley, to serve the red, white and blue, came with a price. For the first time ever, I faced my parents to give them the news. Mom took it the hardest as she wiped at tears. Pop, true to his nature, gave me a strong hand-shake and sage advice, "Give it your best son. Make us proud."

My two younger brothers stood next to Mom, appearing like silent observers – more curious than solemn. I don’t think they understood the grim concept of war. It must have seemed like a great adventure. Miles barely turned 11 and spent most of his spare time on a home-built wireless telegraph, up in the attic, listening to unrestricted military communications. Paul was only 7 but loved to ride the horses next door at the Miller’s farm and pretend to lead a charge of the Light Brigade.

Miles hit me in the arm, a loving but manly punch, "Hey Buck, you get all the fun."

I looked down at him with a smile, "You stay out of trouble with the wireless, Flash."

Paul squinted up and without warning, hugged me, "Don't go Bucky."

I kneeled down and talked to him with a sympathetic tone, "It's okay, PeeWee, I'm just getting some training. That's all. I'll be home before you know it."

I borrowed Pop's 1938 Chevy to visit my girlfriend, Laura, in the valley. The black 4 door sedan carried me on a sad journey to bid farewell to the only love I had ever known. We had been going together for about a year. Although Laura and I had no plans to get married, it seemed like the next logical step. Pop also lectured me about the fact that everyone's life was on hold until after the war.

I had called ahead so when I pulled into the farm's driveway, she stood on the front porch, waiting for me. We embraced for what seemed like an eternity. I wanted to keep the image of her beautiful face, framed with shoulder length brown hair, etched in my memory forever.

"So it's really time, my big Teddy Bear?"

"Yeah, my bag is packed and sitting in the living room. Pop will drive me to the train station, first thing tomorrow morning."

"I'll keep you here in my heart, every day, until you come back."

"Laura, I'm not sure how long they'll keep me in training but count on it – I'll return."

Holding her in my arms, I kissed Laura while my nose inhaled a sweet scent. I knew this exotic aroma – Evening in Paris - cologne I gave her last Christmas. Then we looked at each other, a certain gaze that needed no explanation.

"Do you have to leave right away?"

"No, I've said most of my good-byes."

She smiled and whispered in my ear, "Good, my love. I'll be right back."

She walked to the front door and stepped inside.

I overheard Laura's voice wafting through the screen door, "Mom, I'm going out for a while with Buck. I'll be back in a few hours."

She tip-toed to the front porch and gently closed the screen door behind her. Laura grabbed my hand and we raced to the car. Once there, I headed for the trunk while she slid into the passenger's seat.

I pulled out the plaid quilt Mom put there to keep warm on cold winter drives. Under my breath, I thanked my mother.

Laura watched me lay the quilt in the back seat with a twinkle in her eye.

After we parked in a quiet spot, I felt ripe emotions and wanted to overwhelm Laura with my desire, to infuse and satisfy her with all my lust. I also sensed her passion reaching out to me, drawing me into her pool of bliss.

*****

In the back of my mind, I remembered our first time. At Senior Prom, we danced every dance and Laura looked radiant in her pink gown which seemed delicate as cotton candy. She bragged about her new Cuban heels, snuggling her head on my shoulder, for the first time.

While we glided around the dance floor, other classmates moved aside to let us turn and spin and anticipate each other's step. The two of us seemed like magnets, highly charged and inseparable, while the sound of Glenn Miller filled the room.

No longer able to subdue our biological urges, we pushed through the gym, decorated in pink and blue crepe paper, and scurried to the car. I drove to the top of Tuscarora Mountain and without any hesitation, ran my hands over her ample breasts. Her firm nipples screamed, "Take me!"

I managed to open the binding zipper on Laura's gown while kissing her lips, throat, and then moving down to each breast, in turn.

I helped remove her frilly dress, trying not to tear it while draping the material onto a near-by tree. She laid there with yearning eyes and teased body, begging me to continue and bring her ecstasy.

I struggled to remove my pants and descend on top of her as desire consumed me. As I entered her sacred place, she moaned, while my pleasurable burden exploded, too quickly.

She cried after and then apologized for being too easy - fearing I might not respect her. Caressing her quivering body, I reassured Laura - I still cared. We used the small dome light overhead to dress by, while exchanging glances and small talk. Later, she snuggled next to me, in silence, as I drove her home.

We satisfied each other's needs over the following months, but my growing concern about a possible pregnancy and forced marriage, compelled me to find help. I asked my friend, Big Mike, Tamaqua High quarterback, for some rubbers. Big Mike always bragged about a long line of female conquests and his stash of rubbers.

*****

Memories of our first time faded as we lay in a hot, sweaty heap, our bodies drained of the pulsing lust consuming us only minutes earlier. Kissing her, I consoled, "I love you so much, Laura." She nuzzled close but seemed quiet," What you are thinking?" I asked.

Starting to sob, she revealed, "I love you too, but you'll be gone for a long while. How will I survive?"

"Hey, hey, look at me. The AAF says I'll get leave right after my training. Then we can be together."

"I know, but will we have a future? I want to get married and have kids."

"Laura, Uncle Sam needs me. So many soldiers have put their lives on hold. But you and I, we will survive this war. Let's just enjoy the moments we have now."

With our sexual desires fulfilled, we cuddled for a time. Later, as I drove to her farm house, we traded few words.

I walked Laura to the front porch, wrapped my arms around her and whispered, "Promise to write?"

Looking forlorn, she responded with a somber, "Every day!"

A long kiss sealed our parting and sadness filled me as I headed down her driveway. Before pulling onto the road, I looked in the rear view mirror and saw her crying.

*****

All of a sudden, clapping of hands stirred me to the presence of airmen, including me, seated before Major Bennett. I watched him step from the platform and checked my watch. Hell, he must have talked for at least thirty minutes. However, lost in my own thoughts, I remembered little.

The Training Sergeant stepped to the podium and announced, "Okay, okay, settle down. As of 0600 tomorrow morning, all of you will start to process out. You have three days to turn in firearms and any other military issue equipment. Hey, last but not least, pay off your bar tab at the NCO club. We will be taking inventory on day three so let's get this done.

"Also, since you'll be going on leave from here, transportation has been arranged to your current address. Men, it has been a pleasure serving with you. Good luck in your new assignments. Tenn-hutt! Diss…missed."

Chapter 2

Home for Christmas

I boarded the cargo plane bound for DC on a crisp morning, even for Las Vegas. Pausing for a moment, I scanned the horizon, taking in the craggy, snow covered mountains and brown scrub land. My temporary home for so long, it seemed alien compared to the rolling green farmland I grew up in.

Tugging at the duffel bag and a carry-along, I hoisted them and shuffled into the belly of a drab cargo bay filled with other airmen. The rows of seats appeared time worn from heavy use. Reaching some open chairs, I nodded to a Private who seemed engrossed in reading his letter.

"Excuse me…anyone sitting there?"

He looked up, "I don't think so."

I dumped my bags in front of the seat and settled in. It felt uncomfortable and we hadn't even taken off yet but I didn't care. This plane offered me the first leg of my trip home.

About thirty minutes later, the aircraft started to taxi out to the runway. I waited until it cleared the ground before closing my eyes and letting exhaustion claim me. I welcomed some well deserved sleep.

Sometime later, I woke to the high pitched drone of aircraft engines most likely trimmed for maximum cruise. I also felt a nudge on my arm.

"Sergeant, hey, Sergeant, you got a light?"

I turned my head to find the letter-reading Private poised with a cigarette dangling from his mouth.

Clearing my head, I chuckled, "You know, with the fuel-lines running inside here, your cigarette could blow us all to hell."

"What? You afraid to take a chance - maybe we die today, maybe not. Who cares…do you think for one minute, we're all coming back from over there?"

I looked into his eyes, far too serious for someone appearing even younger than me. Inhaling the air around me, long and deep, I sensed nothing toxic floating through the bay.

"You need to lighten up, Private. You'll burn-out before we finish this war."

"Oh, I plan on being around at least long enough to walk on the Führer's grave. I'm in the Services branch of this man's Army. I'll ship all the pistol packing ammo you can handle to get the job done."

"Well, since I'm in Army Air Force gunnery, it's good to know I have your support."

For the first time, he smiled, "Glad to help. Now…about that light."

"Okay, okay, just stay away from those fuel-lines and don't let the pilot see you." Searching for my lighter in the carry along, I flipped it open and ignited the tip of his Chesterfield as he took a long draw.

Standing up and stretching, I asked, "Have we reached Illinois yet?"

"Nah, last I heard, we're somewhere over Kansas."

I walked down the aisle, nodding to each of the soldiers. Sometimes I'd stop to talk about the war, home, girlfriends - anything on their minds.

An older looking soldier sat near the bulkhead. He sported the rank of Master Sergeant, a reflection of someone who has made a career of the U.S. Army. He seemed engrossed in reading papers pulled from a manila envelope.

As I walked by, he glanced up, "Going home, Sergeant?"

"Yeah, I'll spend some time with my family for Christmas. How about you, Master Sergeant?"

"Me? No, my orders don't allow for any personal time. My family will have to celebrate Christmas without me. Right now, the Army needs me more. By this time next week, I'll ride herd on a passel of Shermans, headed straight into action.

"You have a woman waiting for you, Sergeant?"

"A girlfriend. Our relationship is on hold for now but I suppose we'll get married after the war."

The Master Sergeant lamented, "Let me give you a few words of advice – you're going into war. As long as you're over there, most of the values you grew up with don't count anymore. Back up your buddies, because you'll need each other to survive and don't get obsessed with your girlfriend. I've seen my men receive too many "Dear John" letters. If it's serious, she'll be waiting for you. Live for today, stay flexible and take advantage of everything that comes your way, because when it's gone, it's gone."

Wow. I didn't expect such a raw assessment of what to expect while over there. Sure, we all received orientation training but this was seat-of-the-pants guidance that never made a text-book.

"Thanks for your advice, Sergeant. I think the Nazis will regret declaring war on us. And next time you hear B-17s overhead, I'll probably be on one of them."

"You take care, Sergeant, and I hope it works out for you."

"What's that?"

"The girlfriend."

"Oh, yeah – thanks."

I paced back to my seat and settled in for the rest of my trip. Opening the carry-along, I rummaged through magazines, writing paper and other personal items for my orders. The thick manila envelope hid at the bottom, most likely because I had reservations about reading it.

If the Master Sergeant can face his future - head on - I can too. Nervous but eager, I pulled the sheaf of papers into the daylight. Most of the forms described my personal information except for several papers stamped - Active Duty Orders.

They stated in specific terms that on January 15, 1943, I will report to the USAAF Air Base outside of London. Beaming with pride, I stared at the form where it listed my occupation as "tailgunner".

All right, so I looked at my orders - nothing scary here. This adventure starts after I spend the holidays with my family and Laura.

Laura? Oh my God. What about Laura? I'll be gone for…for a long time. How does a guy know if his girlfriend is true blue? I can't just read her mind or outright ask her. And what about her old boyfriend, Reggie Middleton, from eleventh grade? He bombed out of the physical with a heart defect. Now he's 4F and staying behind. He just might try to steal her away from me.

Enough! I don't have time to wonder, what if? I'll talk with Laura and let her know how I feel. The rest is up to her.

For the rest of the flight, I read magazines, wrote a letter to one of my friends from air force gunnery training and cat napped. The miles slid by until a voice announced our pending arrival at Washington National.

I stowed my gear and experienced a rather smooth landing over the Potomac and onto the north runway. The airport seemed busy with military aircraft parked in the snow on both sides of the strip. We deplaned down a portable ramp and headed across the tarmac to the terminal. Before everyone went their separate ways, I said a few hasty good-byes to my fellow passengers.

I found my way through the busy airport, filled with military personnel of all branches and rank. I wondered how many were headed to the war or going home to enjoy precious time with family.

Reaching the street level in front, I ran through wet slush and hailed a cab to Union Station across town. The streets filled with dirty icy ruts and heavy traffic but not a snow plow in sight. Almost twenty five minutes later, we arrived at the train station.

Stepping past the classy marble and Dorian column fascia, I walked through the cavernous station filled with its perfectly aligned wooden benches to the ticket counter. Several flamboyant Christmas trees decorated otherwise drab and sparse areas. Unlike Washington National, the train station bustled with civilians as well as military.

I booked a ticket to Tamaqua on the 404 leaving at 1630, about a 40 minute wait. I decided to board early and write some more letters. The gangway to the faded black passenger cars seemed lightly populated and the hissing of steam engines filled the air. Piling my baggage on the seat next to me, I grabbed pen, paper and started to organize correspondence to friends.

Progress on my mail halted when travelers started to barge down the passenger car walkway, filling the seats around me. Men dressed in suits, women with their children in hand and servicemen from all branches.

As the passenger car seemed to reach near full capacity, a pilot, also wearing the 8th AAF patch plus the traditional officer's Crusher Cap and overcoat, stopped and eyed the seat facing mine. However, it felt awkward when he just stood there.

Anticipating his question, I offered, "Help yourself, Captain. Always room for someone from the 8th Army Air Force."

"Thanks, airman."

"Sure."

As he sat down and opened a brief case, the Captain inquired, "Where you headed to?"

"Home, how about you, sir?"

"I'm on a 2 day pass, returning to the Veteran's Hospital in New York."

"Well…too bad, you're going to miss the action over there, Captain."

The officer didn't respond, just a pained look on his face as he stared at his briefcase.

He started to remove a bottle from his carry-along and dumped two pills in the palm of his hand.

Tipping his head toward me, he offered, "Bottoms up, Sergeant."

Without another word, he downed the pills - dry - as if he had chugged them many times before.

"Whoo! So tell me airman, what does the 8th Air Force have in store for you?"

"With any luck, I'll help deliver some surprises right on top of der Führer's head."

"Well...that's an ambitious goal, Sergeant. I know a lot of good men will die before you get that far."

Without another word, the Captain pulled out a newspaper from his case and started to read, ignoring me.

How rude, I thought, but then, he paid for a ticket to ride through, just like me. No courtesy required. And if he lives in New York, I expect the Captain lost his manners there.

I finished my letters; then folded, enveloped and stamped them for mailing in Philly. Leaning back in the seat, I closed my eyes and tried to get some rest.

Although I reached some level of sleep, a sense of caution kept me from shutting out the background noise of metal wheels on rails or the presence of an unsettling figure sitting across from me.

After a troubled nap, I opened my eyes to find the Captain balanced on the edge of his seat, rocking back and forth, a frenzied look on his red, sweaty face. His eyes focused...nowhere.

He grabbed his head with both hands and groaned, "Not again. Not again."

Suddenly, his eyes widened, head swinging from side to side as if looking for some eavesdropper and then stared direct at me.

He leaned over and screamed, "You're going to die. Everyone will die. There's too many Messerschmitts. God damn you, this bucket of bolts won't fly anymore."

Shock, shock ran through me like a raging river, compelling me to react to the pilot's ramblings. I stood up and held the Captain by his shoulders.

"Let go of me. Can't you see the flames licking at my feet? I've got to ditch this P-47 right here before the blaze takes this whole damn plane down. We'll never make it out of France alive."

"Take it easy, take it easy, sir. You're on the DC to New York train. Do you understand? You're not in France."

By this time, other passengers started to notice the commotion and the conductor appeared a few seconds later.

"Oh my God, they strafed Eddie's Spitfire. Get out of there,

Eddie. Black smoke pumping out of your cowling. Too many. Too many for us. Jump, Eddie. Jump…jump. No. No. Noooooo…"

I felt the pilot go limp in my arms as I gently lowered him to his seat. All the irrational energy and fear seemed to drain from his body. My hands trembled and I fought to make sense of what just happened. I dropped to my bench and tried not to envision what he saw in his mind's eye.

During my training, I watched the films of aircraft brought down by enemy fire. The wind pitch builds up to a scream as black smoke streams off the plane - cork screwing all the way to the ground. God, I hope Eddie died right away.

Travelers stared but in a solemn, caring way, not like curious gawkers at an auto accident. We all knew what the Captain has just relived.

A well dressed, middle aged, man trudged up the aisle and stopped in front of the pilot. Clutching a black bag, he touched my shoulder and asked, "Can we trade places? I'm a doctor."

"Sure, Doc, take good care of him. Okay?" He nodded and started checking the Captain. We watched and waited while he collected notes on a pad after each test. When he finished, the Doc checked the pilot's wallet and brief case.

After checking several documents, the Doc shook his head and turned to the conductor and me. "Sergeant, I see you're both in the 8th Air Force. Are you friends?"

"No sir, the Captain kept to himself. He just seemed to prefer the company of someone from the 8th."

"Conductor, do you have a private room and a wireless?"

The conductor responded, "He can stay in the radio operator's room while we contact the main terminal."

I chimed in, "What's his condition, Doc?"

"Right now, he's borderline comatose. His papers say he's a psychiatric patient recovering from combat exhaustion."

Doc and the conductor helped him up while I carried his briefcase. We wound our way through car after car until we reached the wireless room.

As they helped him inside, I handed Doc the briefcase.

"Thanks for your help, Sergeant. Who knows what might have happened if you weren't there?"

"What's going to happen to him, Doc?

"I served in World War One as a medic and treated a few battlefield cases. If your 8th Air Force shipped the Captain back state-side for treatment – it looks bad. My guess, they already administered shock treatment and strong sedatives. We know so little about the human brain. One thing for sure, the VA approved this officer's travel privileges too soon.

"Listen Sergeant, we'll get him back to where he belongs. The Captain's best chance for recovery rests with the VA Hospital.

"I'll let you get back to your seat. Good luck, son."

"Thanks, Doc."

Finding the way to my passenger car, I rode the last thirty minutes to Philly in silence, staring at the seat across from me. I felt older, more aware of the dark side of this war. As I changed trains at the Philly terminal, my mood lightened, thinking of Tamaqua and family. But somewhere in the recesses of my mind, recollections of the Captain, a fellow airman, will always be with me.

Chapter 3

Christmas Tree Troubles

Over three hours later, after scheduled stops near places like Norristown, Lansdale and Allentown, the train out of Philly entered familiar digs - Schuylkill River on the right and Scharfe Mountain towering on the left. Several minutes later, it chugged to a stop at the snow covered, Victorian style, Tamaqua Train Station. I waited for women and children to exit the car before grabbing my bags and walking to the exit.

On first sight, I beheld a warm glow of multicolored Christmas lights, decking out the train platform and near-by houses, bathing the area with good feelings for the holiday.

Stepping to the cold cement, I pushed through a bevy of people engaged in animated greetings - women, hugging, kissing their boyfriends, men shaking hands with a manly pat on the back.

I looked around me for a familiar face - Mom, Pop, anyone. My mind rummaged through a clutter of thoughts about the letter. The one sent almost two weeks ago with all the details of my arrival.

After fifteen or twenty minutes, I started to think they didn't get my correspondence. The once busy platform thinned out to only a few people. Hoisting my baggage and managing a disappointed sigh, I headed for the sidewalk to Broad Street.

Turning right, I saw an unending row of car tail-lights heading to downtown and street lamps decorated in Christmas cheer. Chuckling to myself, I noticed the streets and sidewalks had been cleared of all snow. Not so much for DC.

Approaching Hunter Street, I recognized Pop's car, stopped in the middle of the road and Miles, leaning out a window, waving his arms at a frantic pace. With cars beeping their horns, I ran across the street and hopped in the back seat while Pop stowed my bags in the trunk.

Everybody tried to talk at once while alternating hugs and PeeWee seemed obsessed with touching my Staff Sergeant stripes. Pop occupied the front seat, shifted into gear and turned right at Railroad Street.

As he wound his way up Cottage Avenue, Pop found a parking space across from A&P Grocers. Pop raised his hand and yelled, "All right everybody, simmer down!

"Buck, I tried to make it to the station on time. But you know that bastard, Heim. For the last three months, he owed me $200 after I built a brick porch onto Wanamaker's house. The son of a bitch kept putting me off.

"Well, today I marched into his office and threatened him with a law suit. When I told him the next communication will come from Attorney Bowe, he peeled two, $100 dollar bills off a wad, big as his fist and paid me"

Pop reached over the back seat and shook my hand. "Welcome home son. We missed you and look forward to hearing about training. But for now, we need to buy some groceries for your home-coming celebration."

We walked across the street to the A&P and stocked up on beef roast, potatoes plus some special treats like ice cream. As Pop checked out, I bumped into a high school pal who bagged our groceries. He had polio as a kid and walked with a hobble. Military recruiters classified the poor guy 4F before he even graduated.

On the ride home, all of us, except Pop, sang…or maybe bellowed - "I'll Be Home for Christmas". I watched the lights of Tamaqua disappear behind us as we headed into New England Valley. The moon cast a dim light over the landscape, revealing our neighbor's houses, still in their proper place.

We arrived home around eight and Mom busied herself putting groceries away while the boys hung up their jackets. I took advantage of the time to call Laura. Filled with anxiety, I'd waited for this moment since gunnery school, so much to say. Listening to the sweetness of her voice, I invited my girl to dinner and a show the next night.

Mom heated a pot of coffee on the stove and then made a

bologna sandwich for me. I settled back in my favorite, beat-up Heywood wicker chair, a seat Mom and Pop owned before my time.

Soon, everyone surrounded me and they seemed all ears to savor every word about basic and 8th AAF training. Pop seemed quiet when I explained about missing the cut for pilot school. The huge backlog of candidates overwhelmed the available slots. However, he smiled when I told him about ranking first in my class for tailgunner marksmanship.

By nine, the kids took their leave for bed. Mom, Pop and I drank coffee while talking about a dark, secret side to this war - not seen in newspapers nor heard on radio but the whispers between neighbors based on information leaks from the military. Pop's voice seemed strained as he recounted hearing about thousands dead in England including children, heavy losses of our pilots flying RAF aircraft over the English Channel and France plus imprisonment and extermination of Jews in Germany.

Just before midnight, I climbed the ladder to my old bed in the attic. I looked at Miles across the room, asleep and safe from the lunacy of Hitler. Pulling the covers over me, I welcomed the sanctuary of sleep.

I woke to Paul's annoying voice, "Buck, get up, get up. Mom started eggs and home fries. Pop started early, emptied the furnace ashes and went to work."

"All right, Pee Wee, just hold on a second." Pulling on my pants, I found everyone sitting around the kitchen table.

Baby Victor seemed happy in his high chair.

Mom chuckled, "We decided to let you sleep-in this morning. Now, the boys and I have already planned the day. After breakfast, Miles and Paul will spend some time ice skating at the Ressie. Pop's truck sits out front, so you can take me into town. I have a few special things to pick up."

Miles chimed in, "Buck, I have a surprise set-up for Christmas Eve. No one knows and I'm not giving any clues so you'll just have to wait until then."

"Hey Flash, no hints? Come on...animal, vegetable or mineral?"

"No way, Buck. I refuse to give you a tip-off."

"Okay, but I'll keep asking."

After Mom and I finished the dishes, we headed to Tamaqua's shopping area. As I parked in front of Sears, Mom confessed, "Buck, I don't know if Pop told you but since President Roosevelt declared war, bricklaying jobs have been sparse. Companies want to hold off on new construction until they figure which way the war goes. Can't blame em but it leaves only the little jobs. Until this war ends, we'll be living from paycheck to paycheck."

"I have three months back pay with me, Mom. If you need some extra money for Christmas, consider it yours."

"Thanks, but you know Pop, he's been independent all his life. Your father won't accept money from anyone, not even you."

I followed Mom through Sear's narrow aisles, watching as my mother pondered an item's price and then placed it back on the shelf. A short time later, she selected five meager items, placed them in her cart and checked out.

While at the hardware store, we ran into Game Warden Landers, who lived across the street from us. In a gruff voice, he asked, "Your boy, Miles, did he spend any time down in the pine preserve last week? Someone cut the tops off ten Spruces on government land. My guess - to sell as Christmas trees. I received a tip about your boy, he might be involved. You let Miles know, I'll be keeping my eye on him."

Mom trumpeted back, "I know my son, Mr. Landers. He studies hard in school, practices Morse Code on his hand built telegraph and helps take care of his two younger brothers. He has no time or interest for such mischief."

On the way home, Mom confided, "Buck, in my heart, I believe Miles puts all his effort in the things he loves. But he's been gone a lot after school and seems to avoid the subject."

"Well...I've been around long enough to know - you can run into trouble anywhere. But this accusation won't touch Miles, not now - not ever. And what about Lander's so-called tip? I'd like to know where it came from.

"You know, Pop has created some enemies in Schuylkill County. He speaks his mind when someone is in the wrong. Just maybe an old adversary wants revenge by taking it out on Miles."

Mom smiled and touched my arm, "This family needs you, son. I understand why you have to fight Hitler and his Nazi thugs. But with your father looking for work every day, I struggle to pay the bills, care for the boys and keep up the house. Life seems harder without you."

"I know, Mom, but it won't last forever - you can rest easy, I will come back. And in spite of the trouble coming Miles' way, it seems to me, you can lean on him, if the time comes."

After arriving home, I carried the shopping bag to Mom's bedroom and helped with chores. The stove needed coal so I stoked ashes and carried them up the mountain. When Miles and Paul returned from the Ressie, we played several games of poker for match sticks.

As the afternoon grew late and Mom started dinner, I climbed the ladder to my bedroom. Placing my duffel bag on the bed, I pulled out and unwrapped a new Arrow shirt and gray pants. I planned to look dressed to the nines.

Picking Laura up for our date at six, we hugged and kissed as if I had been gone for years. After exhausting our reunion, we headed for the Majestic Theater to watch *Road to Morocco*. Later we enjoyed dinner at the Tumas Café.

"Laura, those pirogues look great, can I have one?"

"Sure, your turkey platter okay, Buck?"

"Not bad, want a bite?"

"Nah, the candy bar at the movies, filled me up."

As we ate and caught up on details of our lives, I thought about the Master Sergeant on my flight home. His words echoed in my mind, "Don't get obsessed over your girlfriend." Although I loved Laura, the fear of a Dear John letter, haunted me. I hated Reggie Middleton, ex-classmate and her former boyfriend. If she strays, it falls on him - the bastard.

Laura and I finished dinner with a round of Pall Mall cigarettes. As we relaxed and continued our discussion, I felt compelled to say my mind.

I held her hand and revealed, "You know I love you, Laura but I have to be honest. I've had a chance to witness some terrible things. Once I join the violence of this conflict, I might not come back or worse."

Pulling away from me, she grated, "Stop scaring me, Buck. I don't even want to think about it. You have my love and I'll wait for you. The rest, I'll leave in God's hands."

"This war has me all spun around, Laura. I don't want to lose you but we can't pretend our lives will be exactly the same when this conflict ends."

"What do you want from me? If I spend all my time thinking something bad will happen, it will drive me nuts."

I looked into her blue eyes and whispered, "Laura, I give you my word, after the war, if fate sees fit for us to be together, I will marry you."

She smiled and responded, "You promise?"

"I promise."

*****

On the day before Christmas, Mom received a call from Game Warden Landers. After hanging up the phone, she sighed, "He found Miles carrying a pine tree on New England Valley Road. Until Landers finds out where it came from, Miles sits in the downtown jail."

Mom and I headed to the police station and confronted the game warden. "Mr. Landers, I want to see Miles. We need to settle this, right now."

He nodded to one of his henchmen and then faced Mom, "Your boy has no proof of ownership, Mrs. Remke. Unless someone can vouch for him, I believe he stole the tree."

Several moments later, my brother entered the room. Mom hugged him, straightened his unruly collar and then consoled, "Miles, the game warden seems to think you stole a pine tree. Tell me what happened."

Miles looked angry as his words dripped with sarcasm, "Landers wants to pick on me instead of earning his money by finding the real thieves."

Landers appeared snooty as he retorted, "Mrs. Remke, the tree has no markings and sits about the same height as the stolen county preserve trees."

Miles bellowed, "I bought it from Mr. Miller, the farmer

down the road apiece. He grows pine trees on the back acreage. I earned the tree by working chores for him after school, but can't prove it until someone fetches him."

Landers broadcast an unemotional stare at Mom and informed, "I dispatched one of my men to the Miller farm. We should know soon. In the meantime, I'd like to share some information with you."

The game warden threw a thick folder of reports onto his desk. Landers divulged, "Several hundred trees have been stolen over the last year. Mrs. Remke, you need to know, a serious felony has been committed here."

Before he continued further with his accusation, I recognized Mr. Miller as he greeted my mother. The farmer stood at least six inches taller than the game warden which made Landers' impending dressing down all the more sweet.

Mr. Miller had the stance and demeanor of a John Wayne. He appeared relaxed and cock sure of himself as he instructed, "Let the boy go, Landers. No need to distress the Mrs. any further. Miles earned that tree by cleaning my barn, baling hay and feeding the horses.

"If you had checked with the forest service, all of us might be tending to more important matters rather than wasting our time here. My white, soft pines only grow about 6 ft. tall. The government planted their hard pine trees back in the 1920s and stand 30 ft. tall. If you count the rings, you'll see my tree has about four, which makes it less than five years old."

Without a Moment's hesitation, Mom grabbed Miles' arm and walked to the doorway. Before we left, she shook Mr. Miller's hand and with a grateful nod, uttered, "Thank you, thank you for your help. Please give my best regards to your Mrs."

The farmer responded, "My pleasure Mrs. Remke. You have a good boy there. I expect to hear great things about him someday."

Facing Game Warden Landers with a look of indignation, Mom stated with blunt sharpness, "I expect that tree to be delivered to my house this afternoon, no later than five."

When we arrived back home, I found the living room packed with friends, neighbors, Laura and lots of Christmas presents. Miles divulged he had planned the get-together for months. He walked to the houses in our valley and invited every family to celebrate Xmas Eve with me.

The game warden delivered and even helped set up the tree. Sometime during the festivities, Landers must have exited without notice. I never heard anything about him again. The night filled with rich memories of reminiscing good times. It reigned supreme as one of the best Christmases of my life.

Chapter 4

England Bound

Christmas morning found me in the attic bedroom I shared with Miles. As I reached to grab my pants, several empty beer bottles tipped over, waking him.

"Merry Christmas, Buck. Did you have a good time last night?"

Looking across the room, I grunted, "Yeah, guess I owe you one, little brother. And about the game warden, I never thought you stole that tree, not for a second. Pop raised you, hell, all of us, better than common thieves."

"I knew you believed me, even before you said it. Buck, those damn Heim boys, I saw Robert and Peter skulking around the preserve road, more than once. I can't prove it but no doubt – the Heims stole those trees."

Paul poked his face in the doorway and yelled, "Wake up sleepyheads. Mom fixed breakfast."

Leaping out of bed, I grabbed PeeWee and exclaimed, "Time for some head noogies. You haven't had one in months."

"Cut it out, Bucky, I'm a big boy now."

"Uh, uuh. You will always be my kid brother which means – lifetime noogies."

Paul laughed as I chased him into the kitchen with Miles not far behind.

"Good grief, will you kids simmer down. You too, Buck. The baby fussed all night because of the festivities. Little Victor just nodded off a few minutes ago."

Mom scanned us through squinted eyes for a moment then chuckled, "Go wash your hands."

I grabbed the Lava soap and headed for Pop's new water pump in the front yard. Miles and I took turns pumping while Paul played with the water more than washed.

As we sat down for breakfast, Pop wandered in through the back door and hung his coat on one of the many hooks lining the wall. He took his place at the head of the table while Mom started to serve easy-over eggs on top of hash-browns with eggnog, coffee and Christmas cookies. Soon the banter of a family together on this special holiday filled our small kitchen.

During a lull in conversation, Pop volunteered, "In case you're wondering where I've been all morning - old man Povick put 4 tires on hold for the Chevy. With my ration card and enough money saved up, Povick's garage can install them right after the holidays. You know, once January starts, everyone with a ration card will swarm his place."

We finished Mom's tasty meal and headed for the living room with Miles' hard-earned, twinkling Christmas tree. Paul raced ahead and started shaking presents and guessing what might be inside. Mom, Pop and I refilled our coffee and adjourned to the wicker couch. Miles volunteered to start cleaning the dishes.

Paul called out the name on each gift and carried it to the correct recipient. After all the colored papers had been ripped to shreds and appreciation given for the contents, we inventoried each other's presents. All of us received adequate amounts of socks and underwear plus one special gift. Pop received a carton of cigarettes, Mom - a sewing kit, Miles - a Morse Code manual, Paul - a red radio-flyer wagon, Victor –a toy truck and me, a safety razor.

With the excitement of our morning winding down, Pop and I ducked out the back door to sample some of his new cigarettes. Lighting our smokes with my shiny Zippo, we just stood there for a few moments, enjoying the fresh air and admiring snow covered, Scharfe Mountain.

Pop looked at me and asked, "You know the Cassidy's?"

"You mean Bud and Ella Cassidy down the road a piece?"

"Yeah."

"Well…his oldest boy, Frank, has been listed as missing in

action for seven months now. Although the War Department won't verify it, Bud thinks he flew one of them B25 Mitchells on Doolittle's raid over Tokyo. According to the newspapers, they kicked butt, but don't say much else."

"Frank? I hardly knew him; he must be at least 5 years older than me. Sorry to hear about it, though. I hope he's okay and makes it home.

"I won't lie to you, Pop; I might not survive this war. On the train home, I encountered a pilot suffering combat exhaustion from watching one of his buddies shot down over France. Hell, we barely entered this war and it's already claimed too many lives."

"I know all too well, son. Sometimes it seems like yesterday, when I set foot in France with Construction Company Ninety. We build pathways into the fray, only carried a pistol, yet I killed Germans to survive. Over 20 years have passed and now the burden of my generation has fallen on your shoulders."

Pop paused for a moment and looked at the ground. Then he put his hand on my shoulder and with a calm voice, shared his words, thoughts, with me.

"Buck, war will test a man's character, his will to survive. You may find yourself facing overwhelming circumstances. Just remember, this family needs you. So do what you have to, no matter how bad it gets and come home to us. Just come home."

Those words stayed with me, a part of my memory, playing

them over and over, in my head. I had never heard my father so profound. Pop had no idea the strength his remarks gave me.

My final day seemed packed with good-byes to friends, neighbors and bundling clothes. The evening ended-up a competitive game of poker using buttons from Mom's sewing box. Before the kids turned in, I handed out hugs and promises to see them soon. Later, Pop and I listened to his radio for news of the war.

Before day-break, Pop woke me and I tip-toed to the kitchen, hoping not to wake Miles, Paul or Victor. Mom poured coffee and we engaged in small talk. Quick glances at the wall clock make time unbearable. After procrastinating far too long, she gave me a hug and teary good-by.

Pop and I piled into his Chevy and headed down the driveway. The last thing I saw tore at my heart - Mom wiping her tears and waving from the front porch.

We headed south on 309 to Allentown and then turned east at the intersection of Route 22. Before continuing on, Pop and I stopped in an old, weathered looking Sunoco Station for coffee, gas and cigarettes.

As we resumed our journey, I watched the rolling green countryside transform to dense urban homes and businesses. The presence of increasing military aircraft overhead signaled we drew close to my USAAF Airport in New York.

Pop drove close to the main terminal building and

accompanied me to the front reception area. A bubbly young clerk processed my papers while we waited in the lobby. Soon after, a second lieutenant approached us and announced he handled new arrivals.

I turned to my father and lamented, "Well...guess I'm on my way, Pop. Tell everyone I love em. I'll write, often as I can."

Pop shook my hand and responded, "Careful over there, son, and remember, we'll be waiting until you return."

Following the lieutenant to boarding door number 6, I saw Pop across the room and then raised my hand. Pop nodded, as I pushed through the door - a last good-by.

We walked across the tarmac, past assorted aircraft to a USAAF troop carrier plane. The lieutenant instructed, "Stow your gear, most of the crew already boarded. Take off is scheduled for 1400, your final destination - Wendling, England."

Chapter 5

Settling In

Base command assigned our crew to barracks on the west end of the landing strip. The accommodations seemed rather Spartan but we hadn't come this far for the Ritz. The bunks felt comfortable and the sheets looked clean, what more could an airman ask.

After selecting a sleeping rack and unpacking our bags, a Sergeant from personnel ushered us on a walking tour of the base. It bustled with activity, jeeps coming and going, maintenance crews on the tarmac and B-17s, lots of them. After an exhausting tour, our guide led us to the mess hall.

The Sergeant instructed, "All right, this concludes your excursion of the base. Grab some chow and meet me at the main hangar by 1300."

On the way in, I chatted with several of the crew about anticipation of our first combat run. I grabbed a mess plate and loaded up on potatoes, chipped beef, bread and a glass of milk.

In the rush for a chair, I ended up sitting next to our navigator, Perry, a "pretty boy" with an Errol Flynn mustache. He tended to wear his hat cocked a bit more than most and his uniform, obviously tailored.

I questioned, "So Perry, you ready for our first mission over France?"

"Sure, ready as you, I guess. The scuttlebutt I hear from some of the old timers, sounds promising. Resistance has been negligible, no flak to speak of and Luftwaffe activity appears spotty. Some call sorties over France, a milk-run."

"Well, I'll be ready when the time comes. My two Browning 50 Cal machine guns have been field stripped, oiled and assembled so many times, I dream about it."

Lenny, one of the waist gunners, chimed in, "Hey, Buck, how does it feel to be called tail of the pig or as the Germans say it - Heckschwein? I'll bet every rookie Luftwaffe pilot will be gunning for you."

"Well…I'm honored. I can only hope to eventually earn the same reputation other tailgunners have forged. Nothing will equal the satisfaction of starting to add some kills to my record. How about you Lenny? Looking forward to eliminating some Nazi aircraft from der Führer's Luftwaffe?"

"Hell yeah. They may have started this war, but I'll damn well help to finish it."

After venting our opinions in full, we finished lunch and headed for our rendezvous at the primary B17 hangar. A contingent of officers and non-coms waited inside. Chairs had been assembled in a semi-circular fashion, I assumed in preparation for our meeting.

A master sergeant stepped forward and introduced the personnel, "Gentlemen, I'd like you to meet Major Larson and his staff. Tenn-hutt."

We all stood at attention as the Major walked forward. He barked, "At ease men. You've arrived at a crucial time in this war. Up until this year, we've struggled for air superiority over France and have almost no presence, anywhere over Germany.

"This situation will change with every heavy bomber that arrives in England. The RAF will continue night time raids while we plan to conduct all day-time bombing runs.

"We'll start by pin-point shelling of French manufacturing targets, such as aircraft and tank parts, ammunition, ball bearings - anything crucial to the Nazi war machine. Also, don't be misled by the light resistance we've encountered so far. Be alert and consider the experience as training for the day we poke the beehive called Nazi Germany. You'll need it.

"Now, familiarize yourself with my staff – Captain Burke, Master Sergeant Purcell and Sergeant Warren. They will be your chain of authority for all orders that come down from command.

"Our ground crew will load your B-17 with ammunition, bombs and any other equipment you require. Your pilot and co-pilot have been busy performing checks on the aircraft operating systems.

"You'll report here at 0300 tomorrow morning to review your mission orders for the day. We need you in the sky as soon as possible and don't forget - be careful out there."

As the Major started to leave, the Master Sergeant yelled, "Tenn-hutt. All right, take ten, smoke em if you got em. Then we'll head over to the plane so you check your equipment."

The rest of that afternoon, I checked my guns, turret, turret door and perch. Everything worked just like I expected. Even though I couldn't test fire the Brownings until we headed over the channel, my confidence ran high. I finished up and helped the other gunners complete their examinations.

By 1800, our crew finished diligence of all the plane's systems. We headed to the mess hall for dinner and then off to the barracks for some sleep. Each of us acknowledged that 0300 marked an official start to our involvement in the war.

I tossed about all night in a fitful sleep and stepped into the morning about 0200. Donning my flight gear, I joined the team forming outside and waited for Sergeant Warren to arrive. I felt a heightened sense of awareness, just like the moment I dropped my first deer to the ground.

The sergeant marched us to hangar 5A where our handlers had already prepared a staging area. We reviewed aerial maps of eastern France with primary and secondary drop sites. Our targets consisted of an aircraft engine facility and a firearms depot.

Weather conditions appeared excellent since a stationary cold front held the area in stable, dry air. Our pilot, Spencer, loved it, since the B-17 climbed and maneuvered better.

Some-time after 0600, we carried the last of our equipment and documents to the plane. I found my way past the radio man and waist gunners to the rear turret. Stowing my gear, I busied myself pulling metallic link belts of 50 caliber ammo from their containers and stacking them on a rack next to me. Last of all, I loaded the first belt into the right side feed. With the first shells in position, I yearned for action.

Spencer yelled over the loud-speaker for a status check of each station. Each of us gave the go ahead and braced for take-off. I heard Spencer starting the engines, one by one, until all 4 roared with raw power and the airframe vibrated in response. I heard the ground crew pulling out our wheel chucks, allowing the plane to move forward.

Looking backward through the clear tail canopy, I watched our B-17 line up with the runway. Without warning, the engines revved at what must have been full power. The runway slid underneath me at faster and faster speeds.

Within minutes, I watched the earth drop away until only patches of green and brown consumed the landscape. Sensing when the plane had started to level off and the engines throttled back to cruise speed, I concentrated on my

Brownings.

I waited and waited to gaze at the blue of the English Channel. On cue I heard the rasping and belching of ammo being fired at full capacity - a familiar sound of the front and waist gunners testing their Brownings. I rotated my guns downward, toward the water, and firmly gripped the triggers, feeling the explosive power behind each shell.

As the Brownings vibrated in my hands, I thought about my family, Laura and even that poor captain from the 8th Air Force, rotting in a mental ward. I'm here for them.

Chapter 6

War and Fatigue

Once we cleared the channel, our B-17 turned south west, following the coast line. Rolling countryside gave way to numerous small farms and eventually - towns like Le Havre and Caen. Our target, Rennes, had a major industrial manufacturing center which lay straight ahead.

After nearly 2 hours in flight, Spencer yelled over the intercom, "Okay, men, on your guns. Damn it! Get ready, get ready. Now! Enemy aircraft - Junkers, four of em at ten o'clock."

My training kicked in as every muscle stood at edge like a tiger - contemplating and preparing to spring on its prey. It happened fast, no sooner had Spencer finished, than I rammed the Brownings hard right and clutched the triggers as the Junkers hurtled past me.

A barrage of noise filled my ears as I launched the 50 caliber tracers in an arc from right to left – watching - as they chased to catch up, and seconds later penetrated one of the enemy's tail and fuselage. To my surprise, a plume of black smoke trailed from its engine compartment when the plane started to nose dive.

I watched the Nazi pilot bail out seconds before flames burst through his canopy. However, I never had a chance to witness his decent after Spencer bellowed, "Stay alert – they're coming back."

The rasping sound of shells, spit from our waist-gunner's Brownings, trailed behind me. I visualized every gunner on this plane blazing away at those Nazi bastards. But I had my own hands full. Their props screamed past me while the ping, ping, ping of light caliber rounds penetrated the fuselage except for a few shielded areas.

They scattered in all directions as I fought to lock onto at least one. Cursing at my tracers as they fell short, I watched the Junkers disappear from sight.

I exhaled a long, deep breath and felt my tense arms start to relax. Then I mused at how tranquil the sky looked without war and even wondered if those three Junkers flew to the safety of home. Perhaps to help their fellow pilot and fight on another day.

Complacency morphed to intense focus as three dots on my horizon seemed on a collision course with our B-17. I checked the breech of each gun for potential jams and slewed the Brownings through their full range of travel. If they want to continue this fight, I'll give em a taste of hell.

I shuffled about on my perch, in a kneeling position, trying to get comfortable, while the profiles of those Junkers grew larger. The buffeting of airplane props against cold, French air turned louder as they came in hot with guns popping off rounds faster than storm driven hail.

Pop's words, "Just come home," ran through my mind as I waited and waited for their range to close in on 500 meters. I hoped to rid the world of at least one more Nazi threat before this day ended.

My trigger fingers flicked nervously while the Junkers advanced - a hostile band of marauders intent on our destruction. Moments later, I fired long bursts in an effort to bring one of them down. One Junker flew left and another - right. The third plane came at me, straight on, with its slugs pelting my bullet-proof canopy reminding me of locust and their sometimes crazy flight into anything. I returned fire, aiming for its engine and with luck, a fuel line.

This lone Junker seemed intent on taking me out. I wondered how well my bullet-proof canopy held up at close range. In a split second, its front propeller disintegrated and the plane careened downward. Bits and pieces of debris slammed against the canopy and tail section as I turned to protect my face.

When the sounds of collision subsided, I looked around me for blood. After determining I came through unscathed, the canopy caught my attention. It had fractured in several places and black pit marks consumed the whole glass area. I exhaled a sigh of relief - it held.

Spencer, sounding jubilant, announced, "Good job, men. We have 4 for 4. Let's finish the job."

Opening the turret door, I stood up and stretched for the first time. I also congratulated the waist gunners on bringing down those two other Junkers.

"Hey guys, I heard the racket back here when those Junkers came through. You must have really given em a taste of good old American lead."

Lenny smiled and then boasted, "Hell yeah, Buck. You know, between Roy and me, we pulled out all the stops, courtesy of Uncle Sam. How about you?"

"Well, so far, it's been a good day. A very good day. I just hope the flak over Rennes falls a comfortable distance below our altitude."

"We'll soon find out, Buck. Let's suit up and get this over with."

We strapped on the flak jackets and headed back to our stations.

We anticipated Nazi artillery units scanning the horizon for us. Within minutes, our B-17 buffeted about from explosive tufts of black smoke, hiding the metal shards hurtling toward us. The smell so close, it burned my nostrils.

Every gunner held position until our bombardier sighted his target and released a massive load of destruction. I confirmed his hit by witnessing the huge column of smoke rising from the industrial complex below. The day belonged to us.

Chapter 7

Bringing the War to Germany

We survived the mission over Rennes and with every raid into France, grew more experienced. Our team anticipated the enemy and we responded with deadly force. However, waiting for - the next mission, endless delays from bad weather or maintenance to repair airframe damage - drove me crazy.

And the need to unwind from that madness consumed every moment of my off time. At first I wrote letters to Mom, Laura, friends and neighbors. Although baseball never excited me at home, I found a talent for playing short-stop in the afternoon games.

On a chilly morning in late January, barracks security woke me before sunrise. "Hey Remke, assembly in one hour at the tarmac. Bring your gear and don't be late."

"Huh? What the hell's going on?"

"Don't ask me. I just deliver the messages around here."

I shaved, dressed and joined some crew members on the way out of our hut.

"Hey Buck, you know any scuttlebutt? The major's driver says the old man called his staff in at midnight. They've been buzzing around ever since."

"No rumors, Lenny, but I sensed something big going on the last couple of days. Maintenance worked double shifts, installing what looked like new equipment. And, a feeling that our pilot, Spencer, spent way too much time in meetings."

After accounting for our crew, support people jeeped us to the tarmac. Spencer plus his three officers - co-pilot, navigator and bombardier met us in front of the main hanger. A bright winter sun started to poke its head over the horizon as Spencer asked for our attention.

"Good morning, gentlemen. Well, we came here to stop this war Unfortunately, it may take awhile. But today - today - we will bomb the hell out of Wilhelmshaven, Germany. Yeah, you heard right – our first mission on German soil. Command says the Nazis use Wilhelmshaven's industrial plants to manufacture war goods. But the primary target of the day sits in their port area. Submarine yards lay just inland throughout the alcove. Okay, load up; we take off in 30 minutes."

I crawled through the bottom hatch, stowed my gear and took position behind the Brownings. Several minutes later, after inspecting my guns and ammo, Spencer hailed me on the intercom.

"Okay Buck, everything check out back there?"

"Yeah. Tailgunner position ready."

"Good. Listen, agents on the ground say the Luftwaffe has an airbase near Wilhelmshaven. They spotted over 25 active fighter planes. With 91 bombers on this mission, I figure we'll inflict some real misery on those sons-a-bitches. Good luck."

"Thanks, Spencer. Same to you."

Our plane merged with the largest squadron of bombers I had ever seen. We lined up for the runway behind an unending array of B-17s and B-24s.

Once our flying fortress reached cruising altitude, we crossed the channel and headed northeast, skirting around Belgium, Netherlands, and then inland to Wilhelmshaven.

Our lead bombers encountered the first Luftwaffe fighters about 50 kilometers outside the city. They came at us in waves from all sides. This time, from the moment of engagement, I fired in long, sweeping bursts, never taking my eyes off the target.

Spent shells piled around my feet as I took out a Messerschmitt. Its left wing disintegrated while the fuselage spiraled downward. But several more fighters took its place. To my right, another B-17 took out a Junker as it burst into flame.

While I concentrated on firing an avalanche of fatal lead at approaching enemy aircraft, all hell broke out around us. On my right, "Lucky Lizzy" started losing altitude as one of their engines belched thick black smoke. Then another, and another.

Four more B-17s fell just minutes after "Lizzy". I watched each craft plummet nose first toward the ground. With fingers crossed, I counted parachutes, as the airmen jumped. To my horror, not all the crew members made it.

Soon after, all enemy aircraft disappeared on the horizon. A signal to every crew member - Wilhelmshaven loomed near and so did flack from Nazi ground units. I felt elated as everyone strapped on their jackets. We successfully entered German air-space, a hard earned, victorious achievement in itself.

But now, our bombardier had to assume control of his prime responsibility, the bomb-sight. He alone had the power to not only destroy the targets but avenge our fallen airmen.

I felt the plane heave about, accepting the cannon bursts below as the price to show Germany - we're just getting started. Everyone waited for him to release the bombs. When we heard the violent sound of explosions on the ground, we crowded to the windows, looking for destruction below.

The sight overwhelmed my senses as I remembered, one of the objectives included a munitions plant. Our bombardier must have hit it dead center. A broad swath of smoke and fire mushroomed several thousand feet wide and lapped toward the belly of our plane.

Before we had a chance to celebrate, flak hit us so hard, I fell to the floor. Struggling to gain my senses, I struggled toward the center of the plane. Lenny kneeled over Roy, pressing on his chest, trying to contain the blood seeping onto the shell casings.

He shook Roy and checked his pulse. With a dazed look on his face, Lenny stood up, and lamented, "Roy didn't make it."

We limped back to England with damage to the airframe. Spencer complained of difficulty controlling the plane and thought the cables to the rudder might be damaged. All of us cheered when those wheels touched the ground.

I considered our close call a miracle when Spencer brought us back alive. After catching our breath, stowing gear and logging the mission, most of us headed back to barracks. On the way, I stopped by the mail room and picked up two letters.

One came from Mom, which I placed in my foot-locker to read later. Laura sent the other and with zeal, I ripped it open.

She didn't waste any words telling me about her conflicted feelings. The bastard, Reggie, kept asking her out on a date and after unrelenting persistence, Laura gave in. Following a few movies and dinners, he wanted to go steady. She insisted the situation meant nothing to her.

Although Laura tried to make it all sound so casual, I knew she had made a decision. Her future didn't include me.

With no one special, waiting for me back home and surviving the Wilhelmshaven mission, life started to wear on me. Up before dawn, prepare for a mission, gulp down breakfast, complete a mission, sleep and start over.

Some guys bragged about getting away from the pressure by enjoying the cabaret nightlife in London. Like them, I now felt compelled to lose myself in every gin joint and cabaret in London.

Chapter 8

Hardened by War

By early spring, the heavy snows of winter started to recede from the flat landscape surrounding Bassingbourn airbase. New B-17s arrived daily and swamped every square inch of the airfield. And everyone, from the commander on down, knew in their hearts, this allied campaign stood at the brink of destroying every major city in Germany.

During my personal time, I traveled off-base to the trendy West London, where a pint of ale and dancing girls soothed my jangled nerves. For a few hours at least, I laughed and flirted while the rest of Europe went mad.

On a bright morning in mid April, our team assembled in the south hangar for a briefing on our mission. Spencer appeared grim as he divulged, "Gentlemen, our target is Bremen. The RAF has been bombing Bremen since 1940. Now, it's our turn.

"You can see why from this latest map. An inlet from the

North Sea allows U-boats to run all the way south to Bremen. This city hides some of the most active shipyards in Germany. The Nazis also control other prime targets there like steel mills, motor works, and oil refineries.

"Our objective today...Focke-Wulf. You know all too well, they manufacture Fw190 fighter planes for Hitler's Luftwaffe. We'll be flying in, hot and heavy, with 115 (B-17s) to take out this plant. But don't think the mission will be easy. Bremen knows the allies will never stop hitting them. Over the last two years, they constructed numerous anti-aircraft artillery installations throughout the area."

Peter chimed in, "God damn it Spencer, save the fancy presentation for your superiors. You always save the worst for last. How many B-17s does command expect to lose?"

Silence overwhelmed the room for several minutes before Spencer responded, "More than the usual five percent. The old man says ten percent, give or take. Agents have reported over 25 fighter aircraft based near Bremen. Look, we all know the odds and they stink, but if we don't stop these Nazis, who will?"

I rasped, "Other airmen, Sir, who put their lives on the line, just like us. But Pete's right, we just want to go in with our eyes wide open."

Spencer walked to the open hanger doors and pointed to our B-17, "Maintenance loaded six tons of bombs and over ten thousand rounds of ammo this morning. The folks at Boeing designed the best plane possible, according to Army brass.

And every one of you received the finest military training available from Uncle Sam."

Our pilot continued, "Now listen here, everyone. You know what happened here since '40, in the news reels, on the radio and in our briefings. At least in a football game, everybody plays by the rules. The Nazis have no rules except win or die. "Hitler has proved to be a madman. He won't stop with Europe, England or North Africa. The Führer threatens the safety of this whole world.

"God damn it! Don't you understand? They will march into your hometown, kill your family, rape your women and enslave the rest of us, unless we win. Now, get the hell out on the tarmac or report to the day officer for court marshal. Your choice. We board in thirty minutes," Spencer barked.

As the no-nonsense meeting broke up, I retrieved my gear from the rear hangar shelf and headed to our plane. Our entire crew milled about the nose of our craft waiting for the bay door to open.

Lenny groused, "Hey, Buck, you got a lot of guts, talking down to the captain. With Pete, I expect it, he likes to irritate Spencer. But Pete also sports a lieutenant bar unlike you, Staff Sergeant. No offense, but next time, just let them duke it out."

"Yea, I know the protocol between officers and noncoms. But I just spoke my mind, Lenny. If Spencer calls me on the carpet, then I'll worry about it."

Minutes later, we boarded our B-17 and assumed positions

for take-off. My routine seemed almost a sub-conscious effort, up until the fighting started.

*****

Every mission grew more intense, dangerous as we advanced further inside the Third Reich. Names of German cities, once unfamiliar, occupied my daily routine in our strategic planning.

By mid-year, our squadron attacked Hamburg for seven days, leaving massive death and destruction.

Soon after, we mounted one of its largest missions ever, Schweinfurt. We crippled their war effort but also suffered heavy losses.

Over the last six months of 1943, I watched the 8th USAAF mushroom into a seasoned air assault giant. The numbers of B-17s increased substantially with new arrivals from the states every week. By then, I felt that nothing, not even Hitler's Luftwaffe could stop us.

Chapter 9

Ilona - Early Years

"Puszi, puszi, Anya" (kiss, kiss Mother), fighting off the tears in an attempt to keep her departure brief, the eighteen year old, blonde haired, peridot eyed, Ilona László, kissed her mother good bye as she left for her first day at the Music Academy.

A cool autumn breeze sent her wavy tresses askew as she enjoyed a brisk walk from her family's comfortable apartment on Pozsonyi út in Budapest. The prime Pest location afforded a view of the Danube, separating the former two cities from the picturesque hills of Buda to the flats of Pest.

Sounds of children's laughter caused her to stop briefly at St. István Park, recalling happy memories of times spent with her brother, István. Her parents, Judit and Zsolt Kovács brought them to the park to play, after which all huddled together on a big park bench and picnicked; their large wicker basket overflowed with kolbász, rye bread, and milk to wash down mother's apple pite.

Following this hearty meal, while the children played, the adults discussed their successful businesses, argued over politics, and mutually agreed that their families were the highlight of their lives. The proud parents as well as their offspring, cherished these precious moments of family time together.

Judit & Zsolt, both born during 1900 in the Alföld, located in the south east of Hungary, knew each other as children. As they grew up, their close friendship turned into a romantic relationship resulting in their marriage in 1918.

As man and wife, they left their small village and moved to Budapest to open a business. The fruits of their strong union produced a beloved son István one year later and the following year, a beautiful baby daughter arrived, completing this perfect family.

Ilona, their daughter, was gifted with a mezzo soprano voice and talent to play the violin. István was a superior student and athlete. Mr. Kovács grew a successful business and ran a paplan (duvet) factory where his wife Judit kept the books and acted as liaison with workers.

The fifteen minute brisk walk to the villamos (tram) gave Ilona time to think and prepare for this new adventure. "I've been waiting for this moment a long time; I'm a woman now and can spread my wings and study hard, the whole world is mine if I want it to be and I do," she muttered to herself.

Ilona's exemplary school grades and sweet personality ingratiated her to her teachers. Never a doubt was cast that she would receive only the highest recommendations and honors that would open doors to any higher educational institution of her choice.

This and her parent's social status afforded an education to which most women would not be privy. Her Music Academy and István's university completion would exemplify success, not only for themselves, but for their parents' accomplishments so they might brag to their siblings and friends.

"My life's dreams of studying music seems a reality; hard work - yes, but I will do what it takes to succeed. My futùre will be paved by my performance here at the Liszt Ferenc Music Academy and nothing can stop me," she prayed.

Arriving at St. István Körút, with a transfer in hand, she boarded the villamos which ran past the Music Academy.

Riding the overcrowded villamos, enjoying the sly looks of young men, she could almost read their secret thoughts. Trying to repress her own urges, Ilona daydreamed of someday having that special man seeking the most intimate parts of her body - gently touching her breasts, tasting them. She imagined feeling the hardness of his body, finding its way into her moist yielding erogenous zones, in a state of suspended pleasure.

Her cheeks burned beneath their gaze and reality settled in

when Ilona suddenly discovered that she missed her stop. In haste and frustration, her quick movement to disembark caused an awkward encounter with a tall handsome man - scattering her new school supplies items all over the floor of the tram.

Blushing with embarrassment, Ilona rushes to pick up the once meticulously organized materials, until a strong voice issues an apology for his clumsiness. Unprepared for such an encounter, coupled with concern for being late for her first class, she attempts pleasantries by downplaying the accident and rushes to catch the tram in the opposite direction.

Getting off to an eventful start, Ilona's enthusiasm remains at an all time high. Ultimately reaching the corner of Király Street and Liszt Ferenc Square, she stopped to catch her breath and observe the sight before her – the Art Nouveau style building of the Liszt Ferenc Academy of Music. Pulling open the heavy doors and entering a dark paneled foyer, she lets out an excited squeal, "Music Academy, here I am."

She took time to inhale this scenario: the frescoed walls decorated with statues of famous composers, the shiny oak paneled classrooms, the serious looking students lugging their cumbersome instruments from classroom to classroom, the oblivious professors scurrying from lecture hall to performance hall. She pinched herself and asked, "Am I dreaming? Is this happening?"

While walking to her class, a familiar face appeared in the hallway. It was the gallant gentleman who had caused her dismay in the tram; the man who helped to retrieve her parcels as she recomposed herself.

As Ilona stared at him, she realized his handsomeness. The strong jaw, straight white toothed smile and unruly thick, brown hair painted a picture of a fearless leader coming to her rescue.

He took her hand and began, "So good to see you again. Everyone here calls me Professor Szirtes. Welcome to the Academy. I assume you plan to study here? What is your talent?"

"Voi… voice," she babbled, as she awkwardly tried to compose herself.

"Wonderful, if you are in my class, I look forward to helping you."

"Th…thank you professor," the new music student managed to stammer as she felt a deep flush come over her face.

Chapter 10

Ilona's Heritage

Brisk autumn air and one quiet spot in a park near the Liszt Ferenc Academy of Music, offered Ilona a chance to retreat and pour through some events of the day. During a break between classes, a couple of students discussed events which recently occurred in Nazi Germany and parts of Austria.

They mentioned their parents' conversations regarding the destruction by SA storm troopers and German civilians. It seems they smashed glass windows of Jewish people's stores and homes, even used sledge-hammers to destroy the buildings.

"Wow, it sounded like a frightening experience", exclaimed one student.

With a smug look, his friend remarked, "Good for them, the Jews deserved it. They live in our cities, take the good jobs and attend our universities. Kristallnacht is just the beginning; I hear Hitler wants to exterminate all of them."

Ilona felt devastated to hear such horrific talk much less know that innocent people were terrorized and hurt. She hoped and prayed that her deep dark secret would not reveal itself on her face or body language.

*****

She remembered the conversation she had with her mother just two years earlier. They sat together on a warm spring day in St. István Park when her mother divulged, "Dear Ilona, you've reached sixteen, a woman almost, and you need to know something."

"Mother, has something terrible happened?"

"No my sweet, I have to share a deep family secret with you. This concealed information must be guarded and then, when the time is right, you can decide if you want to share it with the man you love and intend to marry. Your father and I agreed that you have matured enough to handle it."

"My dear mother, as long as you, father and István stay well, I can handle anything; please go on."

"Can you picture a very pregnant fourteen year girl, frightened, not realizing what had happened to her swollen body? Then picture her giving a painful birth."

"Oh dear, did you know her?"

"No, your great-grand-mother died before my time."

"You mean - Grand-mother Sára's, mother?"

"Yes darling, an older, married Jewish man impregnated your great grand-mother at fourteen."

"Wait, Mother, you mean my great-grand-father was Jewish?"

"Your great-grand-father and your great-grand-mother."

"But how? Why?" Ilona asked, startled and confused.

"Still a child, she must have been naïve and trusted him, a family friend, I suppose. An out of wed-lock baby would have brought shame and scorn to the family. In 1883, families ostracized unwed mothers especially in a remote farming village where they lived."

"So what happened next?"

"The only alternative involved giving up her baby no matter how painful."

"How dreadful," she wept.

"Your great-grand-mother died giving birth to your grand-mother - Sára. She grew up with an elderly childless couple. At sixteen, Sára married Tibor Vargas, a widower and farmer. They seemed happy enough and within a year, Sara birthed me on a spring day in 1900."

"I suppose it had a happy ending, in spite of all the sadness," Ilona added.

"I imagine, for hard working people in those times and conditions. One more thing, your father and I have a letter from the priest which describes Sára's origin. At some point I will give it to you for safe keeping. Remember, for now, this remains our family secret."

*****

The candid discussion between Ilona and her mother two years ago coupled with the conversation overheard earlier in the park disturbed her to the point of exhaustion. Feigning illness to leave classes early, she returned home, to the comfort of her own room. Trying to process these scenarios, she fell into a troubled sleep. Her dreams soon transported her to an imaginary time and place as she foresaw the likely predicament of her desperate relatives.

*****

"Please hurry Mother," the fourteen year old girl pleaded, "I cannot stand this pain in my belly any longer!"

"Hang on, just a little longer, my child," replied her mother, as she cracked the whip to the galloping horses."

"Why couldn't I tell my sisters about the swelling, forcing me to wear your big dresses to hide it?"

"Hush, my darling, we draw near and then all of your pain will be over."

Arriving by daybreak, prayers and singing wafted over the convent walls. The mother used her last bit of her strength to pound on the heavy, reinforced door. "Please open Sister," She cried, pleading with urgency. "My daughter needs your help!"

A kind face appeared in the doorway, smiling yet furrowed by deep lines, maybe from years of sacrifice and responded, "Well, what happened out here to justify interrupting Mother Superior's morning prayers?"

She looked at the pregnant teen and exclaimed, "It looks like she is ready to give birth right away. Let me help you inside." As Mother Superior eased the pregnant teenager onto a clean cot, she ordered the sisters to boil water and bring clean sheets. Her fate now rested with the nuns and God.

After two days of intensive labor, the young mother gave birth. Since her baby grew too large, inflammation consumed the womb. Her physical condition deteriorated due to an inordinate blood loss.

Mother Superior, concerned about the condition of the baby, secretly baptized her. The nun and distraught mother said their own respective prayers for the young girl. She never regained her strength and died two days later. They buried the girl's body in an unmarked grave, dug by the younger and stronger nuns.

The mother returned to her village, harboring eternal sadness, guilt and a shameful secret. She fabricated a story about the untimely death of her daughter, to family and friends. The mother never divulged her daughter's secret or the birth of her first grandchild.

*****

Ferenc Fejes, an elderly caretaker of the local Catholic Church in the Hungarian countryside, lived with his wife, Ágnes, age 52, who was past childbearing age. Their hopes and dreams of ever bearing a child after countless miscarriages had been dashed years ago.

The kind, hardworking people, helped others and loved their local Catholic church. Ferenc kept the grounds, performed carpentry work as well as maintained the carriages and cared for the livestock.

Ágnes sewed, repaired and laundered the vestments for the priests as well as cleaned the parish and cooked for the fathers. They also helped the nuns in a nearby convent. Ferenc and Ágnes enjoyed their work which distracted them from thinking about the children which might have been.

One evening, after they gave thanks for the blessings of the delicious meal of chicken stew with nokedli, which Ágnes prepared, a knock at the door startled them. Ferenc, whose mouth watered, felt a bit guilty because he thought of the delicious meal more so than prayers. Putting his watering mouth on hold, Ferenc opened the door. In the doorway stood the priest for whom he worked.

"Jó estét (good evening) Father, how can I help you?" Just then, an infant wail sounded from the small blanketed basket on the ground.

"God has heard your prayers, Ferenc, and rewarded you," the priest smiled, placing the basket in the humble man's arms.

Forgetting about the delicious stew and nokedli, Ferenc struggled to contain his elation as he accepted the infant. After admiring the precious bundle for a moment, he handed the baby to Ágnes' open arms.

"One more thing," added the priest," a letter comes with the baby."

"Letter, Father?" asked Ferenc.

"Yes, my son," the priest continued, "You should put it away for safe keeping. It describes the baby's Jewish origin. Please guard this secret until the appropriate time comes for it to be revealed."

From that moment on, they raised Sára as their very own.

*****

Terror suddenly filled Ilona's subconscious as the dream continued.

"Mother, help me, the pain, my baby" she cried out. "I want my baby, please don't give it away."

Ilona's mother stood over her, comforting, "Wake up, darling, you had a bad dream again."

"No, no, I saw the nuns, the priest and my great-grand-mother. She gave birth, suffered excruciating pain and died. I felt it all."

"Ilona, I apologize; if the story of your great-grand-mother disturbed you."

"Tell me true, did the nuns, for sure, deliver my grand-mother Sára?"

"Yes, your grand-mother told me."

"Ferenc and Ágnes, they didn't give birth to her?"

"Correct."

"And as Catholics, they still raised a Jew?"

"Of course, an innocent little baby needed parents and they wanted to be her mother and father. They must have felt blessed with this gift from heaven."

"So everyone accepts us as a Catholic family?"

"Yes."

"Mother, you mean, if I tell my future husband about these Jewish roots, he will understand?"

"Darling, if he loves you, it will not make a difference. I realize, there have been hardships for the Jewish people, but don't let it influence your life. You must keep your eyes and ears open and allow your brain, rather than your heart to make a decision."

"Oh Mother, thank you for telling me the story. I always loved my grand-mother and felt so sad when she died. Now I can appreciate her courage so much more. What happened to the letter?"

"Your father and I have it amongst our important papers."

"I don't know what I would do without you and Father."

Chapter 11

József László & the War

József László considered himself superior to everyone in everything. An only child from working class parents, Péter and Éva László, he grew spoiled in spite of their paltry means. Although raised as Catholic, he later convinced Peter and Éva that his studies required full attention rather than wasting time hearing old religious men with colorful robes rant and rave in Latin.

Mr. and Mrs. László managed a sewing machine business. A number of factories trucked used equipment to their small workshop and, Péter repaired them so their mechanisms withstood a few more months, even years of solid labor.

Budapest had several large factories producing clothing, haberdashery plus leather goods, and fabricating these products required well maintained heavy duty manufacturing apparatus. The repair work required difficult labor, especially as Péter's eyes grew older. His arthritic hands, heavily calloused, stiffened, and his once solid, strong back, began breaking down. This type of work began shifting to younger men who turned around the order faster and cheaper.

Éva worked for a small bakery, waking at three in the morning to prepare the dough for rising and then baked multiple loaves of seeded rye and heavy, dark grained breads. Her specialty included sweetened cakes, filled with apricots and apples. Lifting heavy troughs of dough, peeling and seeding apples and apricots all constituted long and tiring hours which she had little reprieve and even less income. All this - just so József had everything he wanted.

József, a superior student and outstanding football player, caught the eye of his teachers who recommended him for the university. József and his best friend Kovács' attended many of the same classes. István's intelligence exceeded that of József; his IQ bordering on genius. Under normal circumstances, József, felt jealous and pulled mean pranks on any competitor, like, removing critical pages from his text book, pretending to review homework and losing it, or changing answers. He thought nothing of spreading vicious rumors about his rivals. Some which hurt and even ruined a person's credibility. His friendship with István proved more useful than threatening and might provide a bargaining chip in the future.

József found any excuse to invite himself to István Kovács' flat to study. As the two teenagers talked, József grew preoccupied with István's beautiful younger sister - Ilona.

Her young body started to fill out, driving his hormones into frenzy.

Completing his university education detailed József's primary goal. He planned to settle into a comfortable, prestigious position where he did not have to tax himself. Then he intended to marry Ilona. He obsessed over these goals, no matter the cost.

The occupation of Europe by the Germans required all young, fit men to fight for their country. István, conscious of his responsibility coupled with the needs of his country, never hesitated to interrupt his education. He naively promised, "I will return soon, after this brief period is over."

József, exempt from military duty, due to a severe hearing defect in his left ear, finished his education.

As the war ramped up, Ilona's parents closed their paplan factory. Only a few older workers managed production because their young employees had to support the conflict. Many loyal customers living in nearby countries had their own national problems and labeled warm bed coverlets a luxury.

The final blow to Ilona and her family was the official letter informing them that István is missing in action while fighting along the Russian front.

Chapter 12

Hard Times

With István gone, the business closing and Zsolt's diagnosis of cancer caused his wife to suffer from depression. These adversities burdened Ilona, causing her to feel guilt for attending the Music Academy. She felt compelled to take control and support the loving parents who sacrificed their lives for her and István.

She decided to leave school and find a job. Ilona bid farewell to the Music Academy with reservation, it felt terrible, a true hardship. She loved her classes, professors and the whole musical atmosphere.

Ilona declared, "I will find a job and work a short time, at least until my parents recover."

In the meantime, her disappointed voice teacher knew someone who needed a cabaret singer. "Look at the positive;" Ilona told herself, "at least I can use my voice to sing."

And so her talented voice never reached the National Opera House frequented by rich patrons and royalty but rather in a smoke-filled club in Buda, frequented by leering Hungarian officers.

Soon, she discovered, using her mezzo soprano voice to make raspy and sexy sounds, appealed to the patrons. Ilona also appreciated the generous tips from soldiers, over her pittance of a salary, which helped support her family.

József came to her house more often. He appeared to visit her parents and over time assumed István's role in the family. His motive was not unselfish. He sought to gain their favor plus win over and marry their daughter.

Although not happy about her cabaret appearances, he found that profit over-ruled his personal feelings. He determined to find a way to possess her whatever it took.

One evening, after her appearance at the cabaret, a Hungarian officer followed her to the villamos stop where she got off and walked a few blocks home. He grabbed Ilona and tried to rape her.

Ilona's cries alerted József who had also attended the performance, leaving just minutes later. József attacked the officer, punching him like a mad-man until the soldier ran away. In the midst of an epiphany, she saw József as her protector.

In her deepest thoughts, she debated, "Maybe he is the one. I have known József forever. He is my brother's friend and loves my parents like a son. Perhaps, if he might love me, I can try to return his love."

Chapter 13

Courtship & Marriage

József became a fixture in Ilona's household and in her life. He stayed until she went to her job at the cabaret, hung around while she performed and escorted her home afterwards. He worked with his father off and on just to make enough money for drinks and gamble in the back room of the cabaret. He also set aside extra funds to treat her with a tram ride when they spent time together on her few days off.

Showing off became a large part of his conversation, emphasizing an obligation to help his parents rather than occupying his precious time with a job. József boasted, "I cannot find a job worthy of my intelligence and skills. I make this sacrifice for them. In the near future, I will work in my profession, using my university education."

Ilona felt unconcerned one way or another about his rant. She patronized, "Of course, József, you must do what is best for you and your parents. We have long lives ahead of us."

Their daily encounters became a comfortable and predictable habit. She spent hours with József, painting a rosy picture about their future as man and wife - raising children, care of their parents and finding an ideal job. When his mantra grew tiresome, she closed her eyes and smiled.

When alone with her thoughts, the family secret churned over and over. Perhaps the time had arrived to share it with this man who seemed to love her. Ilona wondered, "He has a right to know, if he cares about my family and me, I just hope he can be trusted."

One day, with mustered courage and the time seemed appropriate, she approached him: "you need to know something about me." She proceeded to explain the story of her grand-mother's origin.

No sooner had the words spilled from Ilona's lips, than she realized her mistake. He shot up, staring at her with angry eyes, nostrils flared and heavy breathing. He threatened, "How dare you lead me on, keeping this…this disgusting information from me. From now on, if you refuse me anything, I will tell the police."

With every emotion worn down and feeling frightened, she succumbed, "József, what do you want of me?"

"I have invested a generous amount of time on you. We will marry before the month ends."

Later in the evening, she prayed in the quiet of her room.

She asked, "Dear István, if only you knew how much I miss you. Please tell me I have chosen the right path. I may not love him, but he loves me and promises to take care of us. I feel trapped, a Jew hiding in my own skin, paying blackmail in the form of marriage."

*****

She looked about her - empty pews except for the front row, colorful flowers clustered around them, an awkward, young priest and a man she didn't understand - József.

"I do," Ilona pronounced.

"I do," belched József.

The state now recognized their union as final.

They married in a ceremony attended only by their parents. She missed her dear brother István, in the worst way.

Everyone celebrated the wedding by having dinner in a small restaurant. While Ilona just picked at her food, József ate voraciously and swilled pálinka and wine. On two occasions, he staggered for the men's vécé (toilet) to vomit. His drunken talk echoed across the dining room and degraded her further when he made sexual remarks to Ilona, embarrassing her in front of their parents.

"Please, dear God, let his terrible behavior be just the result of celebrating his happiness, don't let him react like this again." she prayed to herself.

Later, they arrived at her parent's flat and turned-in. She

stood in front of their wedding bed, anticipating a passionate interlude to make up for the evening. The new bride had planned to change in the bathroom and emerge wearing a white dressing gown, symbolic of her virginity. She fantasized József tenderly kissing her as he removed it.

"Lie down, wife," József demanded, "You belong to me and I will do whatever I please as often as I want."

Ilona, beside herself, thought, "I don't know this stranger. What kind of man treats his wife lacking of any respect?"

Without warning, József tore off Ilona's clothes and fondled her breasts until they hurt. He held her down to claim her body. "All this time you ignored my desires, now I will not be denied," he taunted.

"József," she tried to scream as he mounted and throttled her again and again. Never having had sex before, it felt raw and painful while she tried to stop him. József continued to ram his manhood inside her until he derived his own pleasure, then rolled over and fell asleep.

Ilona felt humiliated and frightened beyond belief as she shivered at the other end of the bed. "Did he have too much to drink or will it always be like this? I can't tolerate it again," she thought to herself.

Conditions had not improved since their wedding night three months before; József's extraordinary sexual appetite seemed insatiable He needed to pleasure himself with her body first thing in the morning, again during the day and after she came home following her long evenings singing at the cabaret.

József expected Ilona to fulfill her duty as wife and satisfy his needs. He wielded the secret over her head whenever she protested. Continuing to live with her parents, she found it difficult to hide their volatile relationship. Ilona tried so hard not to scream at him but found it futile.

She lamented, "Dear God, can't he see my disgust and hate? At every encounter, I avoid his touch, presence and smug expression."

During the period Ilona worked, József spent time in the flat or local bars. On occasion he visited his parents to accept their pity. He complained about suffering boredom with his in-laws, lonesome evenings or failure at finding the right job. József's whining instilled more anger towards his terrible wife who dared to leave him all alone.

His mother lamented, "Such a terrible woman, you deserve someone better; a nice educated woman who will cook delicious Hungarian meals and make a home."

After six months of a loveless marriage to this once handsome man, she found it more difficult to tolerate him much less listen to the rant of his high pitched voice. Ilona cringed when he tried to pleasure himself.

His once athletic body, once hardened by hours of intensive football training had since grown limp and soggy. József's new occupation consisted of drinking beer with rowdy Hungarian soldiers, just returned from Transylvania. At 22, József looked 10 years older and Ilona, at the tender age of

21 feared she had no future.

Looking into a mirror, Ilona studied her porcelain skin and high cheek bones. They framed her delicate Aryan face with eyes the color of spring grass. The sad young woman tried to understand why she still looked beautiful since inside she felt ugly. Ilona wept tears of sadness, realizing the bitter hand her short life had been dealt.

The small cabaret, a walk down basement arrangement consumed space in the Buda area. It included a long bar and numerous tables which attracted locals and Hungarian officers. With just a piano accompaniment, she sang her heart out to strangers.

These steamy ballads not only paid the rent, but fostered a psychological distance from her tormentor. Ilona tuned him out even if he showed up to watch.

When performing, this delicate, blonde frau forgot her problems by looking deep into the eyes of her patrons and crooning the songs sung by Kapitány Anni, the famous Hungarian jazz singer. She basked in the applause of the packed cabaret.

While chanting notes, Ilona reminisced about early childhood. Musically gifted, and surrounded by music from the radio and recordings, she sang from the time she first spoke.

After dinner and a long day at the paplan factory, her father played piano, accompanying mother on the violin. Ilona and István sang along. Her parents soon noticed and encouraged her talented voice.

"Sing my little pigeon, sing!" coaxed Zsolt Kovács challenging her range and tempo. "Someday, we will see you perform on stage and everyone in the audience will be captivated." Judit nodded her head and winked, reassuring her that her father told the truth.

Ilona's mezzo-soprano voice showed promise, justifying expensive, private lessons. Madam Kopenski, her voice teacher, reinforced her dreams of singing "Carmen" at the Hungarian State Opera House on Andrássy út. Ilona pictured herself wearing the red gypsy dress as she targeted poor Don José while singing the "Habanera".

Without warning, the moment shattered as Ilona fell back to reality when loud voices surged above her sad song. Slumped at an end of the bar, her drunken husband bellowed, "How dare you look at her body like an ogre? The singer, my wife, belongs to me!"

She knew the routine, drunk and angry, József groused about losing gambling money to the backroom soldiers. She tried to ignore him, but with her concentration interrupted, Ilona announced a short break. She took his hand and patronized, "This way, darling," as she led him to the cabaret kitchen for coffee.

Chapter 14

Anti-Semitic Threats

The war-torn environment in Budapest painted a bleak picture. Terror ruled Ilona's life as she witnessed Jewish friends taken away. According to the state, they shipped all Jews to forced labor camps. However, gentile friends never heard from them again.

A sense of doom blanketed her life as traumatic events unfolded. In spite of her husband's assurances, in the end, she knew József betrayed her brother. Hungarian Army command reported István died on the Russian front. She surmised Nazi sympathizers shot him in the back. Her parents, overwhelmed with grief and despair, passed away within months of each other. A cold realization settled in - Ilona's family now belonged to the ages, leaving her alone.

Unsympathetic to her grief, József demanded more control of Ilona's time. In his mind, he imagined her cheating, causing humiliation. Over-bearing parents convinced him that her Jewish blood might bring Hungarian Nazis to their door.

With fewer moments of sobriety, cowardice dominated his judgment. József's next betrayal brought Ilona's Jewish bloodline to the attention of local authorities. As much as he enjoyed tormenting this little flower, József planned on moving on to someone better. In his mother's words, "A woman who deserved him."

Ilona soon recognized that people treated her differently. The scrutiny from her community grew intense. According to Nazi propaganda, she now joined the ranks of sub-humans – Jew.

"Mrs. László, you must leave the cabaret now," demanded her manager.

"What? Leave the cabaret? Mr. Kálmán, I only started my break a few minutes ago. Besides, you hired me to perform two more hours. Why? My singing? The song? Has someone complained? Please - tell me, I will do better."

"None of those things, Mrs. László," he offered in a demeaning tone, "József gave up your Jew secret and how you deceived him into marriage. Leave - and never return here again."

Shocked at Mr. Kálmán's harsh behavior, Ilona composed herself then gathered her coat and make up from her small dressing room. József waited at home to claim her tip money and indulge in his daily harassment.

"Good evening, my sweet Jewish wife!" He belched in a drunken, sarcastic tone, "How many soldiers did my pretty Jew sleep with for tips? Those Hungarian fighters just might slit your Jewish throat next time." By now, she loathed the sight of him.

His interrogations continued non-stop. With her tip money, he bought more pálinka and demanded sex before falling asleep. Next day, hung over, he sought food and comfort from his parents. All their lives entered a never ending, dysfunctional cycle

People thought to be good friends, avoided her and when confronted, acted unkind. The social circle in Budapest, once a big part of Ilona's life began to exclude her, creating an existence of isolation. She suffered discrimination and exclusion in familiar shops.

"I cannot style your hair anymore, I will lose all my customers," threatened the hairdresser, she and her mother used for years.

Ilona lived in constant fear of anti-Jewish violence on her block, just like reported elsewhere in Europe. She shared concern about Hungary joining the Axis, aligning itself with Germany, just like Bulgaria, Romania and Slovakia. News of the German Nazi philosophy foreshadowed tremendous anti Jewish discrimination which also spread throughout the Balkan countries.

Ilona heard unofficial talk of Hungary seeking preferential economic treatment from Germany and re-annexation of northern Transylvania with the rest to follow. She also heard rumors of Slovakian Jews forced to wear a yellow Star of David on their outer clothing.

The local newspapers broadcast news of Jews from France and other countries, deported to forced labor camps. Even though Ilona's Jewish bloodline came only from her maternal grand-mother, everyone considered her just - Jewish. Jobs and education for Jews dried up. Government issued severe penalties for marriage and sexual relationships between Jews and non-Jews.

She saved every penny inherited from her parents and safely hoarded tips from József. She recalled her father's concern about Hungary's downward spiral toward war. Quotas reduced the number of Jewish professionals and students while Nazis invaded surrounding countries. Her father wanted her safe and away from this part of the world and his brother, Ilona's uncle Gábor, might be the answer.

Chapter 15

Gábor

Zsolt Kovács shared many stories about his brother, Gábor, most notable - football stories. Gábor had the shortest legs of any soccer player on the team; however, with speed and determination, he could outrun any opponent and his kick always scored the winning goal.

Gábor excelled at math and science while Zsolt enjoyed working with his hands. Therefore, Zsolt's father thought it best for Gábor to attend the University. Gábor also liked traveling and dreamed about living in another part of Europe.

Zsolt seemed happy with the decision since studying at the University did not appeal to him. He preferred to run a small business and marry his only love - Judit. He embraced a strong loyalty to his parents and his future in Hungary.

Meanwhile, Gábor made arrangements to study abroad in London; Oxford accepted new foreign students and offered scholarships for travel and study. With vigor, he prepared to leave Budapest and make a new life for himself.

At the station, his mother informed, "I checked the bag to make sure you didn't forget anything. Do you have enough money?"

"Don't worry, I'll be fine, Mother."

The incoming train chugged slow and steady up to the platform. As passengers boarded, Gábor hugged his mother then bid Zsolt and his father goodbye. A short time later, after the conductor announced - all aboard, he tossed his bag on the gangway and stepped to the first stair.

"Farewell…farewell everyone," Gábor yelled, holding back tears, knowing he might never return to Hungary.

Gábor made his way to London, a cultural gateway for the world, compared to Budapest. He reveled in the open lifestyle of post World War One England. During his fortunate arrival in 1921, the British government lifted all war restrictions. Night life burgeoned in London's West End with clubs opening and the sound of jazz giving life a new meaning.

"This is where I belong," crooned this transplanted Hungarian.

He loved football, but they called the game Association Football at Oxford. At the University, Gábor soon realized his language represented a major barrier. However, since his football coach took an immediate shine to him because of his running ability, he sheltered him and treated him as his own offspring.

The coach quickly worked to bring his new protégé up to speed with English which he soon adopted as his own. To fine tune this precious package, he suggested shortening his foreign sounding name of Gábor to "Gabe".

Gabe thrived on expanding his mind and crammed numerous academic subjects into his schedule. When not studying, he ended up on the football field. During free time, he found his way to the West End and absorbed the sounds of jazz.

Listening to the smooth reverberations, he reflected, "This country offers so many opportunities. I will live here and achieve success."

The university years allowed him to mature and discover his passion. Upon graduation he chose to study law. Luck and the proper references offered Gabe the opportunity to socialize and move in the proper circles. Later, a prestigious law firm in Birmingham offered him a position and in his second year, married one of the partner's daughters.

As the years passed, Gabe stressed over the spreading unrest in Europe. He read the papers about Spain's civil war, Italy's Fascist party, and Germany's Nazi regime.

In spite of the events surrounding him, Gabe worked his way up to Senior Partner of his father-in- law's law firm. His wife busied herself hosting parties and events, which included royalty on occasion such as the Duke of York or the exiled Norwegian King Haakon.

Gabe and his wife found themselves reaching a comfortable middle age, not having to burden themselves with children. Countless times, Gabe wished to see Zsolt but a million excuses prevailed - too much work, bad timing, commitments of his wife and the most ominous - the uncertainty about Hungary.

Zsolt seldom wrote but Gabe overlooked this, sending letters or cables whenever he thought of his brother. Included in his posts, he always invited Zsolt and his family to visit them at their country home, just outside London.

With Zsolt and most of his family gone now, he embarked on a mission to save his niece, Ilona in Hungary.

Gabe is worried about his niece in Hungary. He wants her to come to England and he knows that if he has to, he could ask the Duke of York to help him obtain a British Visa. Before he chooses that option, he calls his Swiss friend and Oxford classmate, Karl Brunner, the Executive Vice President of the Swiss Central Bank.

"Karl, old chap, I need to get my niece out of Hungary and bring her here to England. The turmoil in Hungary is getting worse and I am worried about her. Travel is almost impossible and I will go to great lengths to get her over here. You know that we've entertained the Duke of York who will arrange to get a British visa. He could call Winston Churchill himself if he needed to.

"What I see is the only way to do this is to let her come here through Switzerland. I know she had some lung problems and maybe you can get her into a sanatorium in Davos."

"Smashing idea, Gabe, Let me make a few phone calls and get back to you in a day or two."

To Gabe's pleasant surprise, Karl called him back the very same day.

"If she can get a medical report about her lung condition - the more serious it sounds, the better, I can get her a Swiss visitor's visa. I called the Sonnenblick Sanitorium in Davos and they will be glad to have her.

"Luckily, I'm going to Budapest in two weeks to attend a banking conference and I will contact your niece as soon as I get there."

"A visa will be on file at the British consulate in Zurich. But heaven help her if the Germans discover Ilona's plans to reach England. This will have to be planned with care and there is no time to spare."

During this time, Gabe's wife brooded about the whole idea. Her selfish urges never allowed for another woman in their lives. Ilona may be Gabe's niece but the intrusion will interrupt her social schedule. With reluctance, Gabe's wife complies with her husband's plan but doesn't like it.

Meanwhile, Ilona reviewed her meager finances and tried to determine the next move. Should she move away from Budapest, maybe to the countryside where her grandparents lived? She disliked farm life; however, her savings might stretch farther. Bleak as the future seemed, she felt optimistic although it only served a temporary purpose. Her thoughts were interrupted, by the ringing of the telephone.

Holding the clumsy, black receiver to her ear, Ilona announced, "Hello."

An unfamiliar voice introduced himself in German. "Guten tag Frau Laszlo (Good afternoon, Mrs. Laszlo). Sprechen sie Deutsch (Do you speak German)? My name is Karl Brunner; I live in Zurich and am in Budapest to attend a banking conference. Your uncle Gábor who is an old friend of mine wants us to meet. How about meeting at the Gellért tomorrow for lunch?"

Fluent in the language due to her musical training she responded, "Ja, ich sprechen Deutsch (Yes, I speak German). What? You say my uncle Gábor asked you to meet me at the Gellért? How do you know him? Oxford?"

"Your uncle Gábor was concerned about you and asked me to inquire about your pneumonia. We need to discuss your medical therapy."

Realizing that the telephone lines might be tapped, Ilona replied cautiously, "Oh, of course, my treatment. Yes, I will arrange to meet you at the Gellért."

Karl arrived early at the Gellért. He walked about the magnificent Art-Nouveau building, admiring the sculptures. Committed to this mission, Karl wished he had an extra day to soak in the thermal baths. He parked at a small table overlooking the Freedom Bridge, connecting Buda and Pest across the Danube.

He straightened his tie when a beautiful blonde woman crossed the room. Standing in front of him, she inquired, "Good afternoon, sir, so you know my uncle Gábor?"

He stood, and in chivalrous fashion, extended his hand. "Mrs. László, I am Karl Brunner. I've known your Uncle Gábor since our days at Oxford. Let's find a table where we have more privacy."

"A pleasure to meet you," replied Ilona, "although I am somewhat confused about our meeting."

Karl looked around the dining area as if someone might hear him. He waved off the waiter then bent over the table toward Ilona.

"My official reason for visiting Hungary - as Vice President of the Swiss Central Bank is to attend a Banking Conference; however it gives me the chance to visit one of my favorite cities.

"Mrs. László, your uncle Gábor wants you to move to England where Jewish people are safe. He wants to help you get out of Hungary; it will not be easy. He has put together a plan to do this. Gábor mentioned that you've had a serious lung ailment sometime ago. Can you get a medical report that would document your condition? Can you trust a doctor to confirm that you would need treatment? If so, you will be able to obtain a Swiss visitor's visa for the purpose of a cure in Davos. What do you think?

After realizing the shock of his words, she thought and replied, "My doctor is a friend of my parents; he hates the Nazi's for what they're doing and I will ask him in the hopes that he will help me."

"When you have your doctor's letter, you will go to the Swiss Consulate; they will issue a three month's visitor's visa. I have talked to the right people and there will not be a problem.

"My dear, you are most fortunate that you have an uncle who is concerned about your safety and wants you to come to England; thank goodness he has excellent connections and will get you a British visa.

"I know this sounds easy, too easy. What your uncle and I risk here might just be our lives. If the Nazis discover our plot, they will think little of shooting you and leaving your body rotting in the street. As for me, they reserve hanging for notable officials and not even England can protect your uncle.

"I will be waiting for you at the Zurich Train Station when you get to Switzerland. Once you have the Swiss visitor's visa, for the sole purpose of undergoing a cure at the Sonnenblick Sanitorium in Davos, it will not be difficult to get a German transit visa.

"You then have to make the train reservations from Budapest to Zurich and wire me the time and date of your arrival in Zurich.

"Do you need any money? If you do, I will be happy to give

it to you.

"Good luck, Mrs. László, I look forward to seeing you soon in Switzerland."

At the end of their meeting, Ilona thanked Mr. Brunner. She also asked him to send her love to Uncle Gábor. Ilona took a deep breath, gritted her teeth and committed to their dangerous mission.

Once she came home, and before she could change her mind, she made an appointment with Dr. Sípos.

Chapter 16

Visas for Zurich

On the grounds of deception, voiced by József and supported by his family, Ilona agreed to an annulment of their brief tumultuous marriage. Of course, the reasoning he used was based on Ilona's failure to disclose her Jewish bloodline until after their marriage. Ilona did not protest this false accusation but gratefully accepted it as an opportunity to dissolve their torturous legal arrangement.

"Another chapter of my life - over, thank goodness," Ilona sighed, after piling the last of his belongings on the sidewalk cart. She inherited her parent's flat, forcing József to move back with his parents.

With this clean sweep, she renewed the vow to leave Hungary before evil claimed her. Again she mulled the task at hand." How can I pull it off? Germans control everything including travel.

"Jews in west Europe - Netherlands, Belgium and France

must wear yellow stars of David. Also, whispers on the street say Jews moved to Auschwitz and Birkenau disappear."

Finding a confidant seemed impossible, since everyone turned against Ilona after József betrayed her.

"Who can I trust? Do I know anyone who cares about me? Dr. Sípos, our family physician, treated us all over the years. He and my father also enjoyed a close friendship in high school and our families socialized several times a year at Lake Balaton. I must take the chance," she ruminated.

Next day, a frightened Ilona checked into her doctor's office. Sitting in front of his desk, she meekly muttered, "Dr. Sípos, as your patient and family friend, please help me. Yesterday, Nazis abducted seven Jewish families from their homes I feel they haven't quite decided what to do with me because of my long, dead Jewish maternal grand-mother. I can't stay in Budapest any longer."

She continued, "My uncle lives in Birmingham, England and offered passage to Switzerland. He also knows an influential Swiss friend to help me upon arrival. After residing at the sanatorium, I will continue to England.

"At a recent meeting, I talked with uncle's friend and he confirmed - Switzerland represented the safest route. He also told me, I need proper medical documentation to support a stay near Davos."

The elderly physician, trying to absorb Ilona's story, remembered when he delivered her into the world over twenty years ago. Dr. Sípos scratched his white head of hair and thought a few minutes.

"Ilona, do you remember about five years ago, when I treated your pneumonia? You needed constant treatment followed by periodic checkups."

"Of course I remember. My condition approached critical until you stepped in and brought me back to health."

Looking over his bifocals into her tearful eyes, the elderly doctor soothed, "I know all about Switzerland and its sanatoriums. With appropriate credentials and money, I can prescribe a couple of months at Sonnenblick in Davos.

"Sonnenblick enjoys a reputation as one of the best sanatoriums for treating people with chronic lung diseases. I recommend this sanatorium and sent many wealthy Hungarians over the years. They know and respect my reputation.

"I will contact the sanatorium and share your medical history. A chest x-ray of someone with advanced tuberculosis will be substituted for yours. The film and my report will serve as proof, you need treatment."

"Once they have the information, what next?"

"Apply for your Visitor's Visa at the Swiss Consulate in Budapest. If anyone will know Sonnenblick, it will be the Swiss. In a few days, I will receive a letter from the Sanatorium's chief pulmonologist confirming your bed reservation. This coupled with my report and X-ray will secure your Swiss visa."

He continued, "At the Swiss Consulate, you will be asked why you travel to Davos. Your reply - lung problems and two months treatment."

"Okay, the plan appears simple enough."

"Almost but I haven't finished," the father figure and doctor answered, "Do you have hard cash or assets?"

"Enough to live off for some time. Why?"

"The Swiss will not accept anyone who might be declared a ward of the State. Non Swiss citizens without substantial funds risk decline of their visa. The Consulate liaison will ask about your sources of income. You will reply, a small inheritance which allows me to live well for the rest of my life."

"I can deal with the complexities of the Swiss government. However, Germans appear ruthless and suspicious of everyone."

"My dear, you will possess confirmation of your reservation for Sonnenblick, medical report from your personal physician, X-ray showing your terrible lungs and Swiss Visitor's Visa.

"All records come certified and beyond German doubt. With this documentation you will be guaranteed a German Transit Visa. Please understand, no side trips or work, you only travel to Switzerland for treatment.

"Ilona, the Nazis will seize my license and throw me in prison if caught helping you. However, I've enjoyed a full life and shared your parent's happiness when delivering István and you.

"Zsolt and I had a warm friendship throughout our childhood and beyond. All my family's beds have been warmed with the paplans produced in Zsolt's factory.

"I understand your fear. My Jewish colleagues, productive Hungarian citizens, lost their positions in hospitals and universities. They cannot support their families anymore. I hate what those damn Nazis have done to our country. Before we all perish, I hope at least one good man has the courage to remove Hitler from this earth."

Several weeks passed as Ilona gathered paperwork and applied for her visa at the Swiss Consulate in Budapest. The process ran smooth just as Dr. Sípos predicted.

Gathering her courage, she walked downtown to the German Consulate. As she entered their large vestibule, German soldiers stood at attention. They looked intimidating, almost angry, and held slung rifles with fingers caressing the trigger.

Ilona stood in line with a mix of well dressed and average looking people. Waiting for over two hours, her legs ached as she reached the counter marked Transitvisum (Transit Visa).

A stocky, brown haired woman, in German uniform, looked at Ilona without expression and declared, "Papers."

Feeling a twinge of dread, Ilona placed a thick folder into the clerk's open hand. She felt sweaty although the room temperature seemed mild. Ilona took a quick swipe at her forehead, hoping no one noticed.

The clerk led Ilona to a bleak looking office filled only with a desk and two chairs. Ilona's body tensed as a German officer entered the room. Under other circumstances she might be interested in his good looks and blonde hair. However, he represented the enemy, an adversary who indirectly caused every bad event in her recent life.

He offered Ilona a chair and lowered into the other. Minutes ticked by, silence prevailed, as he studied her paperwork. The officer pushed back and squared off like an adversary. In curt German tone, he asked, "What takes you to Switzerland, Fraulein?"

Ilona tried not to fidget as she forced her eyes to him. She took a nervous breath and responded, "Health reasons, I suffer from chronic lung disease and bouts of pneumonia. The documents come from my physician and sanatorium along with a current X-ray."

Without notice the Nazi stood up, ignoring Ilona, and carried the physician's letter out of the room. Ilona's heart rate jumped and she wanted to run. Visions of a brutal death, riddled with bullets from the Consulate guards and laying in a pool of blood, pounded in her brain.

An eternity later, the officer entered with efficiency and threw the letter and official looking paper in front of Ilona.

Her stomach tied in knots. Then he ordered, "Form 27 must accompany all doctor approvals. Sign below."

The fabric of Ilona's existence wilted onto the chair she occupied. Ilona fought to hold the Nazi's pen steady as she etched her name on paper.

He studied her Swiss visa and skimmed through the film. Pushing aside her panic, she waited until he looked up, an unemotional, cold stare and posed the question, "How long do you intend to stay?"

"Two months."

He gripped a rubber stamp and slammed it down on the first blank page in Ilona's visa. Outside, away from curious strangers, she leaned against a building and prayed, "Thank you God."

Chapter 17

Travel to Switzerland

"Farewell my beautiful Budapest, city of my birth and childhood dreams. You've turned your back on me so I must leave," Ilona whispered with remorse.

She took one last look at Szécsényi Bridge which joined the two cities - Buda, with its Rococo architecture along with Pest, the home of opera and operetta.

With bitter tears, Ilona bid her last good bye. She loved this city with its theater, music, Liszt, Kodály and Kálmán. Even the gypsy songs of Budapest's Little Paris. However, with each day, the climate turned more treacherous for a woman with Jewish roots.

On her last day she took the villamos to visit the Dohány Street Synagogue. Her parent used to call it Europe's largest. Ilona slipped in and prayed for Sára, her Jewish grand-mother. Sára's bravery always gave her strength, even now.

Although Ilona never claimed her Jewish heritage, to avoid police registry, those secret meditations with her grand-mother felt inspirational.

"Sára, although I may never pray for you in this synagogue again, you will always remain in my heart."

Upon reaching Budapest's main rail location, Ilona clutched at her single piece of luggage, not wishing to draw attention. She just packed a few clothes and toiletries in case the authorities searched her bag. Clutching a purse, containing all the paperwork, close to her chest, this soon to be ex-patriot stepped onto the westbound train in Keleti Station.

Ilona confided in no one but Dr. Sípos about her trip to Sonnenblick. Her voyage from Budapest to Zurich required passage through Austria and Munich.

To stretch her meager savings, Ilona purchased a third class train ticket. She welcomed the inconvenience compared to the fear of anticipating a knock at her door. Ilona tried to remain inconspicuous, limiting her movements and eye contact with passengers or train personnel. She heard how spies lurked everywhere, ready to pounce on unsuspecting citizens.

Sharing a compartment with strangers, she feigned illness and took care not to speak but nod her head when questioned. Listening to conversations in Hungarian and German, she tried to pick up on troop movements, political unrest and travel conditions to Switzerland.

Some Hungarian Soldiers traveled back to their duty stations. An older man in a business suit reminded Ilona of a smuggler. She wondered about the unseen contents of his satchel, maybe stolen military secrets or other contraband for sale to the resistance?

The ride, long and monotonous, tested her stamina to stay awake. As the train made periodic stops, people departed and new ones found their way to the worn, gray seats.

At any point, a uniformed thug picked random passengers and demanded to see their papers. If they interrogated Ilona, she risked losing her connection, papers or even her life.

As Ilona's train entered the outskirts of Vienna, Swastika garnished streets screamed capitulation to the Nazis. Overwhelmed by the German presence, she took a deep breath before transferring to her next train.

"Papers," shouted an arrogant German soldier who blocked entry to the train.

When her turn came, Ilona offered papers, without a word, eyes to the ground.

"Purpose of your trip, Fraulein?"

She replied in fluent German, "My disease. I travel to Sonnenblick Sanatorium in Davos, as my physician's report shows." She ended the response with a deep, raspy cough.

The Nazi gate keeper to her train took a step back and replied, "Auf Wiedersehen, Heil Hitler."

"Danke," Ilona replied. In her mind, she celebrated with each step onto the gangway.

She found her third class compartment filled with German soldiers and middle aged German ladies. The soldiers tried to engage her in idle conversation, but Ilona answered only in short replies.

The soldiers, young and handsome, tried to flirt, but Ilona avoided the temptation to respond. She pretended to sleep as the train moved along the tracks swaying like a cradle.

A blonde haired sergeant asked her destination, "Switzerland," she replied.

"And what takes a beautiful woman like you there?" He pressed her.

"Doctor's care for contagious pneumonia." she hacked, forcing wet splutter onto the floor. Several ladies exited the compartment and the rest kept their distance.

Several hours into the trip, with her stomach starting to growl, Ilona exited to find the dining car. On her way, she came across a soldier struggling to get off his hands and knees. Shocked by his compromising situation, she helped him up, noticing his crutches and missing leg.

Embarrassed but grateful, the young corporal shared, "Your kindness just saved my pride. These Bohemian kamerads of mine have no tolerance for weakness. Oh, excuse my manners, everyone calls me Hans."

"Delighted to meet you. My mother chose to name me, Ilona, it comes from the Greeks for light and beautiful."

Feeling sorry for this wounded warrior, Ilona invited him to the dining car for coffee and apfelstrudel. She searched for an open spot as they walked past occupied tables lining the wall. Ilona noticed patrons staring at him as they filled a booth near the kitchen.

They enjoyed a meal together and talked, while she studied his innocent looking features. Ilona wondered how such a fragile man came to this terrible end.

"A Russian mortar shell exploded within eight meters of us. It killed three of my kamerads and shattered my leg. As you can see, they amputated it just above my knee.

"Now, I plan to visit my fiancé, Gretl, in Bavaria and afterwards my parents. My army career ended in Russia so I will live on my family's farm near Lake Constance in Southern Germany."

"What kind of farm?" she asked, trying to keep him distracted.

"A few acres of wheat, eight cows, two horses and a few chickens. My parents expect me to run everything but now it will be impossible, first losing my older brother and now my leg."

"Lost your brother? How?"

Tears glistened in Han's eyes as he answered, "His

commanding officer said a sniper killed him."

To lighten the mood, Ilona contributed some stories about her family, their paplan factory and good times in Budapest. Hans laughed aloud at stories about her childhood antics with István.

Throughout her trip, the abhorrent Nazi flags, Swastikas and posters of Hitler cluttered each town's thoroughfare. Ilona, feeling their obvious surrender to Nazi domination, returned to her compartment while the train made a brief stop.

Hans entered the rail station to contact his parents and update progress on the trip. A short time later, she watched him enter her compartment and sit down. A look of shock on his face alerted Ilona, the news had been grim.

In a sympathetic tone, she asked, "Has something bad happened?"

Hans bowed his head and wept, "Gretl married the head of our town council, the Burgermeister. He has to be at...at least 40. Why? She promised to wait."

Ilona reached out to hold him and whispered soothing sounds, "Hush now, and please don't cry, this will pass. She lied to you, so shame on her. Better to know it now instead of later."

Trying to sooth the teary eyed young soldier, she sits closer and they cuddle until the next stop.

During their 3-hour layover at Munich's Haptbahnhof

Station, Ilona held onto his arm as they checked into a small hotel nearby.

Two frail souls looking for compassion and an innocent kiss develop into a passionate encounter. At first, he is embarrassed to unmask his amputation. However, she helps him to forget for a few moments, just long enough to savor each other's warm bodies and pent up emotions.

During the pinnacle of his bliss, he moaned Gretl's name. In an instant, Hans exclaimed, "Damn," rolled on his back and lit a cigarette. He took a deep, long draw and expelled the fumes upward.

"I apologize. You have every right to be angry. I never expected to, you know, say her name."

"You've endured enough pain for any human being. You don't even seem to fear my contagious pneumonia. Believe me Hans, I understand," she murmured.

He chuckled, "At this point, nothing scares me."

As they dressed, Hans seemed happy, even philosophical.

"The war will be over soon, Liebling. I sense Germany rising to victory. Mein Führer fulfilled his promise to dispel the unions and Marxists. Now he reaches out for the world."

Ilona staged a fake smile, thinking of the atrocities Hitler's Germany committed on her family and Hungary. She also reflected on this poor soldier's ignorance of the truth. A nagging question haunted her - how many innocents do the

Nazis control, like sheep?

They returned to the rail station on time for the next link in their journey. Passing the time with small talk, Ilona and Hans arrived three hours later at Lake Constance on the south German border. Strangers but connected, Hans grabbed his bag and bid a tearful good bye. He hoped to meet again but Ilona knew better.

Ilona prepared for the last leg of her trip to Switzerland. As the train made its scheduled stops, German soldiers often steamrollered their way through the cars, selecting passengers at random to show papers. They removed an unassuming man from her compartment and Ilona noted as her train left the station, he never returned.

A new passenger filled the empty seat next to her. He claimed to be a Swiss physician returning from treating a German industrialist in Munich. He felt fortunate to get a third class accommodation since the first and second class seats filled with German officers.

When Ilona offered an introduction, in return he asked her destination.

"Sonnenblick near Davos."

"What a coincidence. I work there. My name is Doctor Sutter."

He spoke to Ilona about past adventures and shared ample fare of cheese, brown bread and beer.

A Swiss flag greeted their arrival at the St. Margareten border. Ilona, bone weary, disembarked and planted her feet upon neutral ground. She resisted the urge to kneel and thank God for her safe arrival.

She freshened up a bit in the station washroom and then stood at the taxi stand. Dr. Sutter offered to share his ride with her, but she refused.

"Thank you but I expect a dear friend."

She did not want the doctor to see Mr. Brunner when he arrived. No need to arouse his curiosity. Ilona hoped to remain aloof and blend in at Sonnenblick. She felt relieved when his cab drove off.

Sometime later, a familiar face approached her and resounded, "Welcome to Switzerland, Ilona, so good to see you."

"Mr. Brunner, me too," sighed Ilona as she hugged him.

On the drive to Sonnenblick, Ilona started to relax, even as they passed Swiss soldiers on the roadway.

Chapter 18

Switzerland

Ilona filled with awe by the splendored surroundings of the Brunner's Villa. Framed by endless windows overlooking Lake Zurich, it sported a clear view of the snow capped Alps in the background.

"Did I die and go to heaven?" she asked.

A confident, feminine voice answered, "Heaven on earth, darling child, relax and enjoy, long as you wish." The voice belonged to Anna Brunner, Karl's wife.

Anna looked mid 40s, a large-framed woman, whose eyes twinkled as she spoke. Her braided hair, brown with gray flecks, framed a smiling oval face. Anna's robust arms opened to receive the young woman, but Ilona's body stiffened to such warmth and kindness.

Ilona pleaded, "Forgive me if I seem to be stand-offish. I've lived through too many terrible things. Perhaps in time I will come to terms with it."

"My dear, we've looked forward to your visit from the beginning. When Gabe… your uncle Gábor, told us about making arrangements for your passage, we prepared a room."

After Ilona's warm reception, she walked outside on the lavish wooden porch surrounded by an ornate banister. Looking in every direction, she admired the openness.

She thought, "I appreciate my new-found freedom yet still sense the stark fear of hearing someone pounding on my door at midnight. My nightmare continues with vulgar soldiers raiding the apartment and marching me to a God-forsaken place.

"Whispers on the streets of Budapest rumored of German Nuremberg Laws legitimizing death camps. Sometimes I can almost smell the stench of their Nazi hell where starvation, brutality and death wait for me."

Anna, being a gracious hostess slipped into the kitchen and reappeared bringing fresh drinks and chunks of delicious cheese and rye bread

"Here…here, a toast to Ilona - one brave woman, and to her new life. Please enjoy the day, roam the grounds, rest in the comfort of your room or indulge in my library of classic works. In other words, take this time to freshen your mind and body. Anna will bring your meals in-room. We can regroup the following day," Karl suggested.

Ilona laid her head on the snowy goose down pillow perched on top of the soft inviting bed. Memories crowded her mind, fragments that brought certain events into sharper focus. She daydreamed about her family's holiday weekends on Lake Balaton.

She loved the train ride, sitting near a big window, watching the world outside and listening to the clickety clack of the rails. Time flew by in an instant before you realized half a day passed with Lake Balaton just ahead.

Her family loved wearing bathing suits and splashing in the crystal clear lake. Her parents relaxed, laughed and appeared to savor this time together.

She reflected, "Please grant me one moment to hear their voices, feel wet from the lake and hug them one last time."

István and Ilona played hide and seek near their villa on the north shore of Lake Balaton. He found the best hiding places which frustrated her to tears, "No fair, big brother, you hide better than me."

Sensing her distress, he appeared in an instant, bellowing a devil-may-care laugh. He stood two inches taller with mischievous green eyes. "Don't fret Ilona; I'll never leave you alone." A big hug followed with all forgiven.

When visions of József appeared, she fought to push away this unhappy period of her life. "I can't dwell on the past. The voyage to England has just started and needs all my energy."

The following day, she awoke, bathed and felt like shouting to the mountains, "Nothing can stop me now!"

Soon after, Anna announced breakfast awaited their new guest in the dining room.

Ilona felt overwhelmed when she saw the broad array of scarce food: eggs, coffee, fresh milk, meat, bread and jam.

"You must have used most of your ration stamp allotment!"

"We treat the local farmers as friends and pay them well for their dairy products. Most people around here do this. The coffee, we enjoy on special occasions like now. Please eat, enjoy, for after breakfast we have many things to talk about."

She indulged in the fresh foods denied to her for so long. After the delectable meal, Ilona struggled to move. Settling back and gazing at her empty plate she noticed a brown folded paper next to it.

Ilona questioned, "What have we here?"

"A telegram, it has been waiting for you some time. Please read it," ordered Karl.

Skeptical as well as curious, she opened the envelope, "Uncle Gabe, Uncle Gabe," she yelped with joy, "I can't wait to read it."

*****

In Hungarian he wrote," Kedves Ilonkám, Hihetetlenül boldoggá tett az újságod hogy ide fogsz jönni lakni. Nálunk bár meddig maradhatsz, az extra szoba mindig várni fog rád. Köszönd meg a Brunnerékat helyettem, hogy Ők ilyen kedves házigazdák voltak a részedre. Sok szeretettel várunk. Gabe bácsi".

*****

Dear Ilona,

I can't tell you how happy we feel that you plan to stay with us in England. Our home will be your home for as long as you wish. Please thank my dear friends, the Brunners.

Your loving Uncle Gabe

In the evening, Karl and Anna surprised their charming guest with a ticket to the Zurich Opera House. "For me," surprised Ilona questioned, "How magnificent, opera in the summer."

"My dear," responded Karl, "we have a box reserved. An easy task when you have the proper connections. This performance will feature "La Boheme", one of my favorites."

Ilona beamed with enthusiasm, "I love "La Boheme" also."

"Such peace, I can walk amongst these Swiss citizens and not feel someone looking over my shoulder. People laugh, children play without fear," chirped Ilona to Karl and Anna.

"Darling child, you might have perished in Budapest. For the sake of humanity we felt compelled to help you escape. It gives us such joy to have you here. As for your uncle Gabe, he extended a helping hand to us many times over the years."

*****

Karl rescheduled a few meetings to plot Ilona's itinerary for the next link in her journey. With map in hand and a list of destinations, he laid out the strategic route.

"Our first step will be to pick up your visa at the British Consulate, followed by Spanish and French Consulates."

"Why so many?" questioned Ilona.

Karl explained, "While Europe wages this damn war, every country looks on travelers as possible spies, saboteurs or defectors.

"A word of caution when you travel through Vichy France; you must prepare for heart wrenching sights of poverty. Nazis have arrested most of the men in unoccupied France and shipped them to Germany. To harvest their crops, women of all ages work the fields.

"Also, Spain struggles to recover from their civil war of 1939. Don't be surprised when you see rubble, shacks and debris from the bombings.

"This, my dear, explains why all the paperwork must be in order, allowing you the best chance to pass in safety.

"One last caveat, your final transfer will be a Spanish freighter, the Atlantico, which will take you to an English port."

"Freighter? What kind of cargo will it carry?"

"Bananas from Spain."

"I love bananas," she giggled.

"Even better!"

For the next few weeks, aside from obtaining the necessary visas, they exchanged life's stories and enjoyed music, dining and good friends

*****

With good bye hugs and kisses from Karl and Anna, Ilona boarded the Swiss train to Spain. She felt sad to leave these caring people and their beautiful Switzerland with its breathtaking ambiance.

Ilona with her three visas safely tucked away, prepared for the long trip to England. In spite of her protest, the Brunners insisted on giving some money to tuck away in case of an emergency.

The trip to Seville took three days of unexpected stops, stretching her patience to the limit. At least the Brunners purchased a much appreciated second class ticket which insured a more comfortable ride.

"I hope the hard part lay behind me and my transition to England will be uneventful," Ilona reflected.

However, her opinion changed when she observed the depressing contrast of France. Passing through some of the rural areas, she saw the rubble of farm buildings and the rotting remains of crops, just as Karl predicted.

She recalled the Brunners discussing France's Jewish population, men, women even children herded into cattle cars, and sent to Auschwitz. Trying to repress those horrific scenes from her mind, she fell into a fitful sleep.

A loud bellowing voice awoke Ilona and alerted her to a stop at the Spanish border. The comfortable Swiss train she enjoyed continued on to Madrid. She had no choice but complete her trip on a Spanish train to Cadiz.

Arriving in Spain, she observed first hand, the obvious poverty. Ilona waited in a run down, filthy rail station until her train arrived. The crowed passenger cars looked the same, patrons smelled unbathed and mothers tried to soothe their screaming babies.

She adjusted to torn seats with sharp edges and minimal storage areas. The fly encrusted food looked inedible and one of the two toilets refused to flush, leaving its nauseating overflow on the floor.

"Think of England, think of England, think of England," Ilona kept whispering as her train chugged forward.

After two intolerable days of her traveling prison, the train finally arrived at Cadiz and a step closer to freedom.

The banana freighter, Atlantico, already sat in port. Ilona presented her papers to the purser and climbed the gangplank. Searching around the gray, confusing vessel

Ilona questioned a seaman, "Private cabins, please." He pointed to a narrow stairway below deck. It led to a large room with several narrow bunks. Not the private room Karl booked and paid for.

Near the wheel house, a plethora of different languages filled the air - spoken, shouted or argued from mouths of every nationality. Overseeing the chaos stood a yawning Spanish gendarme wearing a three-cornered hat and appearing bored.

"My God, no privacy, no understandable tongue, how will I survive?"

From the isolation of the aft deck, Ilona observed the purser account for each passenger as they boarded. Soon after, the captain announced, all Atlantico hands must prepare to leave port within the hour.

Using coins for bribery, she obtained clean linens and a warm blanket. Ilona also secured an empty locker to protect her steamers.

Determined to make the best of bad circumstances, Ilona came on deck and observed the rolling waves and groups of people walking about. Realizing this voyage may also be a challenging part of her journey, she set her mind on how to deal with the rowdy crew and noisy disgruntled passengers for the next four nights.

Chapter 19

England - Birmingham

Atlantico docked at Liverpool without fanfare, ending Ilona's bristled anger, aggravated by days of cold showers, questionable meals and forced isolation.

Ilona's original simple suitcase was upgraded to two steamers, housing lovely clothes and shoes, courtesy of Karl and Anna Brunner.

She recalled the Brunner's final words, "Just remember if your plans in England fail please return to Zurich."

Such a kind gesture, but now, Ilona reached out to England and family. In her deepest thoughts she wondered what Uncle Gabe looked like and if he might recognize her.

After packing her clothes in the trunks and supervising their delivery to the deck, she joined the other passengers strolling down the gangplank. She wandered among a cluster of people rushing to greet the fellow travelers.

Ilona stopped in her tracks when she spotted a face in the crowd. A well dressed gentleman resembling her father walked forward. All her emotions took wing as she ran to his arms.

"Oh my God, Ilona, I suffered a thousand deaths, thinking the Nazis took you or the Spanish rabble held you for ransom. But now…now you have arrived, safe on British soil."

Staring at him, she realized Uncle Gabe represented her last family member. Ilona savored the moment, since this might never happen again.

"We must hurry, my dear, your aunt waits for us at home. I've also made arrangements for your trunks to be delivered," uttered Gabe in Hungarian, "You will have your own room, bath and any other comforts needed."

Gabe ordered his driver to take a scenic route for part of their journey. He and his niece chatted while parks, statues and historic buildings passed by. The Nazi Blitz destroyed many parts of the city so he avoided them. He wanted Ilona to feel safe and forget about her traumatic past.

Over three hours later, they arrived at Gabe's home. The housekeeper greeted them at the door and the driver retrieved her steamer trunks.

"Take them to Ilona's room," ordered Gabe, "the one facing Handsworth so she can enjoy the view."

She stood in amazement of such a big house. Gabe showed

her each of the five bedrooms with their own bathroom.

"This area dwarfs three of our rooms in Budapest, and we considered them big."

Ilona reasoned, "Father mentioned Uncle Gabe's success, but he never imagined this."

"Freshen up and come downstairs," Gabe hollered.

Before joining him, she donned a new hand-knit sweater. During her stay in Zurich, Anna completed several of varied color and design. For her first night in England, she selected a dark green pullover with plaid skirt to match.

Descending the long spiral staircase, an aroma of roast beef greeted her sensitive nostrils. Granted, she ate the same meal in Zurich, but it never smelled as good.

The marble steps ended in a large foyer decorated with what looked like two large Ming Dynasty urns.

"It appeared Uncle Gabe and his wife either shopped at the best import firms or traveled abroad. From my studies in Budapest, I recognized some works of art from the Orient and Middle East. I must request a tour of this magnificent house, but had better wait until I settle in."

"Oh dear," came a loud feminine lament, "I missed the arrival of our important guest."

Gabe's wife, Elizabeth, stepped into the room. An overweight, middle aged woman, she wore a stylish suit and heavy make-up. Elizabeth also showed discomfort, pulling at her waist, maybe from a tight girdle. Ilona sensed this woman wanted to give the appearance of someone younger.

Elizabeth, eying this Dresden doll-faced woman, forced a smile and hug. In a monotone, she welcomed Ilona to their home.

"Dinner is served," announced the cook.

Uncle Gabe and Ilona followed Elizabeth into the dining room. As they sat down, helpers served the aromatic roast beef, Yorkshire pudding, roast potatoes and sponge cake with dried fruit. Tired and hungry, she fought the urge to stack her plate with food but instead remained lady-like.

During dessert, she presented a box of Lindt Chocolates purchased during her stay in Zurich. Everyone devoured them in short order since England rationed the sweets.

Next day, Gabe took her on a walking tour around Hilltop to enjoy the scenery and catch up on her life.

"Please tell me about the last years of my brother, Zsolt, I miss him. He almost never corresponded, but I wrote him many letters over the years. I wanted to let him know, I never forgot."

At first, Ilona recounted a few happy memories and tried not to dwell on the last few months of her parent's hardship. However, as she talked, words and events seemed to flow unrestrained.

Gabe's niece detailed the anxiety filled days, waiting for

news of István and learning of his death in battle. She even reached into the dark recesses of her mind and exposed the unpleasant marriage to József.

She felt relieved to talk, cry and even laugh. Ilona perceived a bond forming between them but sensed a cool, distant feeling from her aunt.

"Now, we must prepare for your future, maybe entering a music conservatory or university? I have the means and influence to help, no matter what you decide. I make this promise in your father's memory.

"Since we have no children and my wife comes from a wealthy family, aside from my favorite charities, you embody my only living heir. I will set up a trust fund with my Solicitor, making you the sole beneficiary.

"My dear Uncle Gabe, please, you have done so much over the years, sending gifts of money during the holidays, not to mention my tuition and even the Brunners."

Holding her close, like a daughter, he responded, "Ilona, you alone hold the future of our blood-line. I've reached the fall of my years and Zsolt, Judit and István belong to the ages. With you here, in England, the next step in my life stands clear as the sky above us. If this makes it any easier, please accept whatever means I've accumulated as your moral birthright."

*****

As the weeks flew by, Elizabeth grew more apprehensive of

Ilona. Gabe added to the tension by adoring her to excess and in return, his wife's tolerance turned to paranoia.

Elizabeth pondered, "Gabe helped her flee the Nazis, an admirable thing. But now she continues to live here. What does she want? Ilona can't just interrupt our lives without consequences."

Ilona settled into British life, trying to speak English at every opportunity. However, her language skills suffered even with a tutor. Fluent in the tongue of her homeland and then Zurich left her with only a smattering of English from cabaret songs.

Elizabeth challenged Ilona's language at every turn. "I don't understand Hungarian or German. You live in England now, when will you learn to speak English?" Of course, her uncle never heard these sarcastic comments.

Feeling the strain between them, Ilona thought of leaving this beautiful setting. She did not want to be held responsible for ill feelings between the couple.

"But I have no plans of my own for the future. I remain a stranger here with little money, no work credentials or friends. Of course, war, bombs and queuing dominate the news. Everyone waits in long lines for food and material rations. How do I defend my existence for the most basic supplies? And my uncle will ask why I choose to leave, how can I tell him?"

Taking advantage of a neutral person, Ilona decided to drop hints to her English tutor. Such intimations included, "How does one travel to London with public transportation? What jobs might the city offer? Which sections offer affordable flats?"

Her instructor listened with interest, but he also wanted to remain employed. After all, she started to make progress which made him look good in the eyes of his employer.

The tutor deflected her questions and offered an impartial, "The first step to success in London demands perfect English."

With serious effort, Ilona began to speak English in short sentences and only spoke Hungarian with her uncle.

Gabe maintained his conviction regarding Ilona. As the last László in his clan, by succession, everyone will recognize her right as heir. However, he procrastinated in planning to tell Elizabeth of his decision.

"No need to bother my wife with the details right now. I'll just draft the document, submit it to my partner for legal review and sign it. Then she can confirm it as my witness."

A few days later, when Elizabeth answered the phone, senior law partner and close friend of her deceased father, invited Elizabeth for tea. Curiosity getting the best of her, she agreed.

Next afternoon, she journeyed to Barrister Row. The firm looked unchanged, British architecture with thick oak trim and decadent furnishings. She sat on a plush settee while the family friend poured black tea. Elizabeth took a sip and placed the cup on a near-by coffee table.

"Betty," blustered the senior partner, "I remember you as a toddler, watched you grow up and marry our brightest partner. You and Gabe okay?"

"Yes, why do you ask? If you have something to say, just give it to me."

"My dear, I received an unusual request from your husband. He drafted a will which he wants me to finalize for signatures."

"Well…since we both have sizable estates, Gabe and I never felt the need for one. With advancing years, I imagine he just wants to arrange the proper disposal of his assets. The dear man always looks after my welfare."

"Hold on Betty, before you go any further - the will does not include you. It provides for his niece alone, leaving the entire estate in trust for her."

"What!" she exclaimed in disbelief, "I knew it. Gabe has been brain-washed by his devious harlot. Ilona plans to push me aside and take over. She wants his…our money." Elizabeth bolted out the door, ignoring her tea and buttery biscuits.

Back home, Elizabeth exhibited a Jekyll and Hyde personality, caring and pleasant or aloof and critical depending on Gabe's presence. Oblivious to actual circumstances, Ilona felt her aunt had just grown impatient with the slow progress in learning English and local customs.

Even as Ilona polished her English, Elizabeth grew more unpleasant. The time had come to share her feelings with her uncle. In her mind, Gabe's wife unleashed abuse for no good reason.

Waiting until her uncle arrived home from the office, she appealed, "Can we take a stroll through the green. I must talk with you right away."

"Of course, my dear, just give me a minute. Elizabeth wants to chat about something, so I'll be in the library."

Pacing back and forth in the living room, Ilona flinched when she heard Elizabeth and then Gabe shouting.

"I've dedicated years of my life to you. This - nothing - plans to manipulate you and take your money. I want her out of my house - now."

"How dare you intimate something tawdry? Don't try to smear my niece's reputation like a King Cross tart."

Elizabeth went on to confront him about the will and trust he intended to set up for Ilona.

"You have three times the assets which will more than provide for your comfort. I've been successful and now my turn has come to pay it back. For the memory of my brother and his sacrifice, he stayed behind to care for our elderly parents while I attended Oxford.

"I won't tolerate your jealous and selfish behavior. Tomorrow, I'll give this…this unethical partner of mine bloody hell for betraying confidence between lawyer and client."

As Elizabeth opened her mouth to respond, Gabe gasped, "I can't breathe."

He fell to the floor with a loud thud, grasping his chest.

Depressing muted light drifted through the hospital window, as Elizabeth and Gabe's doctor stood next to the lifeless body of this once successful barrister.

"I've listed the cause of death as an acute myocardial infarction. Had he been under any unusual stress?"

"Since his Hungarian niece moved here several months ago, he seemed irrational at times, hiding things from me and confrontational too," she grated.

In her room, Ilona wept over the passing of her uncle. Now, she was the last László remaining of her family.

Chapter 20

Struggle, Salvation and Opportunity in London

Reeling from the gut-wrenching devastation of her uncle's death, Ilona endured the sad and elaborate funeral. She knew she lived on borrowed time in what had been Uncle Gabe's house.

Her life spiraled downward within days after the guests and visiting dignitaries departed. Elizabeth moved Ilona's personal items to the maid's quarters in the attic, forced her mealtime with the help and fired the English tutor.

Sounding more like a stranger than an aunt, Elizabeth issued an ultimatum, "You will not feel comfortable in this house any longer since your uncle has passed. I'll arrange for your shelter elsewhere, say, in London? From what I hear, public transportation appears adequate and factory or service jobs abound in the city.

"My driver will take you and your trunks to some modest hotel. I'll also cover your board plus a few pounds for food and transport for two months. This satisfies my obligation to you and your uncle.

"I have Gabe's estate to deal with so - complete your packing by day's end. If we don't meet again, it has been most interesting."

She turned her back to Ilona and marched out of the room…and her life.

Packing her steamer trunks with care and weeping all the while, she ruminated, "Uncle Gabe, you died protecting me. Thank you. But now I've been cast out and it all seems like a bad dream."

*****

Settling into urban life soon turned intolerable, compounded by her relentless frustration with communicating. Although Ilona's English had advanced, her accent and slow tempo remained a barrier. Therefore, finding a job continued to be elusive.

Her sheltered life in Budapest with doting parents and brother or even the dysfunctional life as wife to József, did not prepare her for living alone in a foreign country.

Brushing aside the dusting of snow on a park bench, she sat with her head bowed and began to weep. Nearby, an elderly gentleman spotted Ilona and attempted to console her.

"I say there, m'Luv, why's a pretty little thing like you crying so hard? It breaks the heart of an old bloke like me, you know. Take this hanky now, go on, blow good and hard."

Looking up through salty tears, she noticed his kind smile, calloused hands and neat but worn clothing.

Offering his hand, he initiated, "Please Luv, call me Mike. Most days I pass through here just to get away from the flat for a bit. Cooped up I say. And who might you be?"

"Ilona. Pleased to meet you, Mike. My…my life seems to have gone astray."

They struggled to communicate but with some effort he understood her plight and suggested a kitchen job might be available in the cabaret where he worked as a cook.

"With food rationing during this ghastly war, they just keep me because I make common potatoes look like the king's banquet.

"As for your hotel, in these times, it can be dangerous for a young woman alone. My wife and I have a spare room in our flat. A bed and dresser take up most of the space but at least we have a secure shelter. The room belonged to my son, damn Nazis killed him, and our house seems so quiet and empty now. Care to give it a look-see?"

Ilona, holding back her tears, let out a boisterous honk into the thin, clean handkerchief. She swallowed the lump in her throat and replied nodding, "Igen, (yes), köszönöm, (thank you)."

With his arm around her trembling shoulders, Mike

shepherded Ilona to the modest dwelling he shared with Mary, his wife. Ilona inspected the room and although tight, found it to her satisfaction.

The couple felt overjoyed to have their vacant room occupied with a young person, filling the emptiness of a beloved son who will never return.

*****

Ilona's life now consisted of dragging her tired body to work, washing mountains of dirty glasses, plates, pots and pans in hot water and harsh soap. The once perky blonde had been replaced by skin and bones. Her soft skin was dried and scaled like an unused alligator suitcase.

Even though her body ached, she never complained. Ilona's good-natured spirit made her a favorite in the large working kitchen.

"I am - he, she, it is - you are," Ilona whispered, "kávé - coffee, kenyér - bread, bor - wine, vécé - toilet, I will learn English, even if it kills me."

She continued to learn new words in English, some not so nice, but it didn't matter, at least she progressed toward fluency.

As time went on and her comfort level with the cabaret personnel increased, she started singing at work. The kitchen staff enjoyed Ilona's sweet voice and even taught her a few vocals of the street.

During one of her songs, Niles Morris, the club's manager popped in to request a special dish for an important customer. He happened to catch her rendition of an aria from "Carmen". To confirm his immediate impression, he dropped by several times and then asked to speak with the new dishwasher.

Ilona, who now spouted phrases and intelligent sentences, told him about her vocal background.

As a result, he requested a private audition. Ilona put on her best dress, air dried her thick wavy blonde hair and dabbed the last tube of red lipstick onto her lips.

Niles met her in the owner's private office. Mr. Templeton owned several cabarets throughout London and hired singers who had talent, looks and brought in business.

Servicemen liked to frequent these places and spent a lot of money when payday arrived. One of the larger cabarets on the West End of London needed to replace a singer who just reached her third month of pregnancy.

"Show us what you can do," Mr. Templeton requested.

Ilona sang several Hungarian songs from her favorite Hungarian jazz singer Kapitány Anni. Kapitány Anni sang these songs where she would switch from Hungarian to English. And Ilona memorized all of the words and included them in her private audition. To show off her range, she jumped to the lively aria where she appeared flirtatious as she sang, "Musetta's Waltz" from "La Boheme".

"By Jove, girl, where did you ever get those lungs?" trumpeted Mr. Templeton. Although impressed with the quality of her voice he hedged on making an offer because of her limited English.

However, after noting the disappointment on her face and overriding his own judgment, he suggested she spend some personal time with Maria, the pregnant singer.

"Perhaps she can coach you on English songs and how to create a stage presence."

*****

During the next few months, Ilona spent every free moment working with Maria. The Hungarian transplant and pregnant chanteuse struck up a close friendship. Maria taught her flirtatious tricks which seemed to work with men.

"Keep this in mind, ducky, look deep into their eyes; let them long for you as you croon sad songs. Make them like you and you'll earn bigger tips. Servicemen have money to squander so why not spend it on you?

"Yanks feel homesick for their wives, girlfriends, even their mums. Your performance has to reach them all. After a while you can pick and choose, depending on the customer's pocketbook.

"On break, let them buy you a drink. Ask for champagne but warn the bar tender to only serve soda water. Remember, you must always remain sober and in control.

"Also, I'll show you some easy make-up techniques. You'll have to buy cosmetics on the black market to enhance your green eyes so they look sexy for the boys. I'll introduce you to my source.

"Push up your breasts, show cleavage, let them desire you, make them want your voluptuous body. Remember, they can look, drool, hunger, want, but they must not touch. A man's imagination is a woman's best friend."

Dizzy from information overload, Ilona tried her best to process everything. She prayed for the strength to hold this façade together, not only to survive, but perhaps begin a new life.

By Maria's 6th month, even the softest draped gowns and tightest laced corsets no longer concealed her pregnancy. Ilona, svelte and sensual stepped forward to take her rightful place.

Chapter 21

Cabaret Singer Meets Tailgunner

Ilona developed a following of servicemen who spent generous portions of their pay for a few pints and the attention of an attractive cabaret singer. Their loyalty produced a steady income and nest egg.

When the time felt right, she rented a convenient flat on Brownlow Mews, West End, a short distance away from Mike and Mary's flat in Islington. Although the move brought tears to all of them, the couple understood how Ilona had to find her own way. She promised to visit every day and share details of her performances.

As a creative seamstress, Mary introduced Ilona to the popular rag and second hand clothing shops. From remnants, bits and pieces of this and that, she fashioned lovely gowns for the new chanteuse look.

Ilona paid Mary for her effort which produced an endless supply of evening dresses. Mary, in turn converted their dead son's bedroom into a sewing room. With this new-found career, the elderly woman no longer had to rent it out.

The bonding of this couple to Ilona created a semblance of family she needed. "You and Mike have been like parents to me," she confided, "I believe you saved me from the life of a bawdy street walker or worse."

With teary eyes, Mary replied, "Luv - I believe God sent Mike to rescue you from the dark side of this city."

*****

She enjoyed singing to the servicemen, but cautiously remained unattached. Ilona remembered Maria's words, "They go off to war and maybe die in battle. If they return, it will be to their wives and girl friends, never to you - never...to...you. They lust for a woman's touch, her scent, her body, her sex. Any indication of interest on your part will either cause tears in their eyes or a bulge in their pants or both. You owe them a good performance, nothing more."

*****

Ilona observed young soldiers looking virile in their military uniforms. Their maturing bodies peaked from intensive physical training. She imagined some of them had already seen the violence of war, fighting for their lives, dodging a hail of bullets and tending the blood soaked bodies of their buddies.

These fighters reminded her of her brother István, when as children they played war games and he threatened, "Bang,

bang Ilona, I killed you."

"No! You missed me, István. I won't die, you can't make me," she retorted and then cried.

He placed his arm around her and consoled, "Sweet little sister, in a battle, soldiers always die, but we don't have to play…any more. Not if you feel so sad."

She felt incapable of knowing the true depth of their pain, but the sting of her make-believe encounter with death felt no less traumatic.

*****

One evening, during a performance, she noticed a handsome but forlorn American airman in the audience. He appeared a bit inebriated which most considered normal in a cabaret. What stood out about this young man rested in the fact that he came alone, during the week. Most airmen arrived in groups on the weekend, if not on a mission. Ilona's heart started to tug with compassion the longer she stared at him. The serviceman's sad face and simmering hazel eyes seemed to reach out to her.

She wrapped up with one of her favorite songs, "We'll Meet Again" which continues "Don't know where, don't know when, but we'll meet again some sunny day." The song describes soldiers going off to war and the hope pf returning. Well knowing that many soldiers of course did not survive. Of course, the meeting place of an unspecified time in the future might be seen as in heaven.

No sooner had Ilona given her usual courtesy bow signaling the start of a break, than she strolled over to the compelling Air Force serviceman. Leaning over his table, she tried to distract the young man and soothe his presumed pain.

"You have a name, staff sergeant?"

"Walter Remke, Jr. What can I call you, ma'am?"

"I go by Ilona. Tell me, why I haven't seen you around here before, flyboy. Missing that girl back home?"

"Pining for a lot of people ma'am - family, friends, anyone I care about. But since the war, I spend a lot of time thinking about Nazis. The ones I sent to hell."

"What do you mean, Remke?" Her voice accelerated an entire range, "You seem too young and sweet to hurt anyone."

When Ilona looked at him, she saw a tall, lanky kid, like someone wearing their older brother's uniform and playing soldier.

"Ma'am, I risk big trouble for telling you this but I ride the tail of a powerful bomber. When Nazi aircraft dare to threaten the back of our plane, I unleash fire and damnation on them. I've succeeded in bringing down almost every Messerschmitt and Junker in my sights. My efforts help insure our fortress can reach its objective and reap a harvest of overwhelming destruction. What bothers my soul; I see no end to it."

Ilona felt humbled by the profound words coming from a mere lad. The war appeared to sit heavy on his shoulders. For the first time she ignored Maria's warning by engaging this man...this warrior, in conversation.

He seemed consoled by talking to this attractive blonde singer, now sitting across from him. Even to the casual observer, it stood evident - a spark had been ignited between them.

He tapped a Camel cigarette on his Zippo lighter. As Remke lit up, he inhaled a long draw and asked, "Your accent doesn't sound German, perhaps Romanian?"

"Hungarian. I grew up in Budapest. Where do you call home, Remke?"

"New England Valley, just outside of Tamaqua, Pennsylvania, a little coal-town in the USA," he blurted out with pride. "And please call me Buck, that's what everyone calls me.

"Ilona, maybe we can share some coffee or tea at a local café after you finish here?"

"Sure, Buck," Ilona answered, accepting his invitation much too soon, "but you'll only find gin joints in this part of the city. I rent a flat just blocks from here. If I brew a fresh pot of tea, perhaps you can tell me all about your family and the little place in America."

Realizing she stepped over the line by ignoring Maria's warning, Ilona reassured herself, "He seems like a troubled but quite sincere lad. Besides, the late hour and lack of cafés make my flat the only logical choice."

Ilona wrapped up her show for the evening and met Buck out front. They walked the short distance, past red brick townhouses with small shops on the first floor. The couple arrived at her building and entered by a side door. Climbing some narrow stairs to the second level, she unlocked her door and turned on the lights, tidying up as she hung their coats.

She poured boiling water over the tea and steeped it before straining the aromatic liquid into white porcelain cups. They sat at the small kitchen table, across from each other, sipping at the steaming brew.

As they engaged in conversation, she hung on his words about the USA, state of Pennsylvania and the (small town of) Tamaqua. The local customs seemed down-to-earth and its citizens lived in safety and harmony. Their loyalty to a benevolent government conflicted with her taste of a ruthless police state. Well past midnight, they ran out of energy and banter. With a kiss on the cheek, he bid her a pleasant good night and departed.

*****

The winter's cold and fuel rationing made her sanctuary an unwelcome place. Ilona lamented, "Better to leave early for the cabaret, at least they keep the patrons warm." She pulled the second hand, fur coat tight around her slender shoulders and walked a quick pace, "This weather feels worse than

Budapest."

Ilona's thoughts wandered to the previous night when she invited Buck to her flat. "I can't do it again, too risky. I live alone and servicemen hunger for the taste of a woman. Who knows what might happen? But God help me, at times, I have my own urges."

Feeling the cold invade her feet and hands, she walked faster and concentrated on the evening's show. Tonight's performance offered several new songs including holiday pieces - "White Christmas" and "I'll be Home for Christmas".

About to enter the cabaret, she saw Buck standing outside. Flustered, she called, "Hey Buck, we don't open for another hour. Waiting for someone?"

"Sort of," the airman hesitated, "I wondered if we might catch a taxi to the Feldman Swing Club after your show. My friends say I dance quite well."

Not expecting such an aggressive offer, she smiled, fluttering her painted eyelashes and retorted, "We'll see. Come inside, I'll have the bartender draw a pint and you can sit up front before the crowd arrives."

Before long, the cabaret packed with airmen. Even though the 8th AAF designated all missions top secret, she learned many B-17 crews had orders to ship out for special action and the rest, left behind to maintain their bombers. As she looked around at their eager faces, Ilona knew she might never see many of them again, so tonight's performance had to be special.

Setting a holiday mood, she opened the show with "White Christmas". After hearing Bing Crosby's recording, she felt it might help the boys take their minds off the war, if only for a little while.

During her break, she talked to a mix of servicemen plus a few locals. Ilona asked them about plans for Christmas. Only a few with injuries said they received orders sending them back to the states. A few airmen joked about celebrating at 10,000 feet over Germany. They smiled and with a wink, marked it up to business as usual.

To finish the evening, she sang, "I'll be Home for Christmas". As her sultry voice resonated through the audience, she noticed some men holding back tears, others staring into space, maybe remembering Christmas past and several left the room. When Ilona crooned the end phrase - "I'll be home for Christmas, but only in my dreams", she prayed, "please let me keep it together, just a bit longer, right through to the end…for these brave men."

Because many airmen shipped out the following week, she tried to say final good-byes to every one of them. At three in the morning, the last few crew members left for their missions.

Since the hour grew much later than expected, she felt nervous about the walk home. At first Ilona thought Buck might escort her but his front table stood vacant. She ruminated, "Perhaps he grew bored or resented my cavalier attitude when he offered to meet later."

Now Ilona wished she had accepted his request. Pushed to face a moment of reality, she admitted feeling a strong attraction to the airman from New England Valley near Tamaqua, Pennsylvania. Ilona wanted Buck to protect her from an imagined boogeyman hiding in the early morning darkness on Richmond Grove Street. If he didn't get her, perhaps a Nazi Baby Blitz might. She whispered a curse for denying her feelings.

On most nights, her manager, Niles, only worked in his office until eleven. "Perhaps he stayed late tonight with the exodus of so many airmen. If so, maybe I can grab a ride home in his shiny Aston Martin."

She opened a door marked - EMPLOYEES ONLY - and entered the hallway. Old pine trim and stucco walls looked faded plus the dusty wood floor creaked with each step, a vast difference from the decadent ambiance out front.

As Ilona approached Niles' work place, she heard voices - laughing, boisterous. She knocked on the frosted glass pane of his door and questioned, "Mr. Morris, can I have a word with you?"

"Ilona? Please do, come in. I thought you might have left but now you can join us in a toast to our and giving the Nazis what-for."

Stepping into the office, her eyes widened as she gazed at him and Buck, sitting around his desk. Buck passed an open bottle of Grant's Whisky to Niles. He reached into a drawer, pulled out one thick glass, monogrammed - Big Smoke - and poured two fingers high of mash. Niles stood up and held the drink out to her.

"Here's to the Yanks who give their all in helping us put an end to this war."

She accepted the offering and clanked her tumbler against each of their glasses.

"Smashing show tonight, Ilona. You sold out the house and left em with a beautiful finale.

"Oh, forgive my manners; Buck says you've already met."

Ilona and Buck nodded to each other. Niles smiled like the Cheshire cat, sensing some unspoken connection between them.

Forcing a cough in an attempt to clear the air, he divulged, "When Buck told me about growing up in Pennsylvania, I had to know more. You see, my Uncle Richard owns a night club on South Street in Philadelphia. As you can guess, night life runs in our family.

"Buck, it has been a delightful evening. Now, I understand why my uncle loves it there. Thank you for introducing me to their way of life - a city filled with such opportunity and enthusiasm."

"My pleasure, Niles. I don't often get to share stories about family or neighbors; much less an account of the hustle and bustle in Philadelphia. I don't feel like a historian but I grew up listening to tales of fighting for freedom which took place in eastern Pennsylvania over 150 years ago."

"Well...I imagine you young people have better things to do than sit around chinwagging. The wife will start preparing breakfast about now so I'll take my leave. Buck, I hope we can talk again."

"Me too, Niles."

They bundled up and headed out a back door to the alley. An overhead light cast a dingy yellow glow over the street. As Niles unlocked his car door, he inquired, "Can I give you a lift?"

Ilona looked at Buck and he smiled back, "No thanks, I'll escort the lady home to insure she arrives safe."

He offered his arm and she accepted. Together, they started to walk back to her flat. Ilona's fear of the night evaporated with Buck at her side.

The couple engaged in small talk about not having enough time to make the Feldman until they reached the flat. Ilona looked at her watch and offered, "Daybreak comes around eight which give us three more hours of darkness. I think we need to make good use of it."

This time, Ilona surrendered to the whirlpool of passion starting to consume her. As they engaged in a frenzied embrace, she also sensed his raw physical hunger.

Behind the snug, boned bra and silky, red gown, her tingling nipples and ripe breasts moaned for his touch. Animal emotions ripped free of their repression. Right now, she needed to be conquered, reducing her loins to a quivering mass.

She ran her fingers through his trim, regulation hair cut and satisfied his wanting lips with sweet kisses. He responded by caressing her all over with his strong hands.

Buck felt the intensity of Ilona's desire as he pulled her close. Her heart beat fast and breathing slowed, deepened.

"Darling," he whispered, "I want you." Buck needed the softness of her pliable body. He slid a hand to her flat tummy and pushed beyond to the essence of her pleasure. By using his fingers with lustful efficiency, he aroused her to the peak of submission, and then penetrated her wet and compliant temple.

At first, he stroked her slow and gentle, building…building in rhythm. Her breath now came in short pants while she begged, "Oh my love, don't stop." Suspended in time, they entered a place where fireworks exploded over and over and over.

Afterward, as they lay exhausted, Ilona felt immersed in a sea of warmth and love. She nestled beside the handsome man who brought her such beautiful lovemaking. In her mind, she slammed the door shut - forever - on memories of the violent sex, once shared with József.

While collecting her clothes, spread all over the room, she teased, "Where have you learned to make love, flyboy? Did you practice on girls in - uh - your little American town?"

Realizing how sarcastic she sounded, a long hush prevailed.

Buck tried to rationalize Ilona's hurtful comment. He shared his manhood with Laura – a half dozen times - and heard no complaints. He reached the conclusion, either she had some unusual sexual need or Ilona enjoyed poking fun at him.

To end the awkward silence, she took back her hasty comment, "My love, don't look so serious. How do they say it in Pennsylvania - I kid you. The truth, from my heart - you have given me pleasure, I didn't think existed."

*****

Ilona woke late-morning and rolled over to find her musky smelling lover cuddled up close but asleep. She rubbed her hand across his chin stubble, and then kissed him.

"Wake up my love, Christmas morning has almost passed us by. I have no present for you except maybe the landlord can be bribed to provide extra heat. Since the cabaret closed for the holiday, we can enjoy this time together."

They spent the morning, soaking in her oversized tub of hot bathwater. At first they engaged in horseplay, spritzing each other with water, and then telling funny stories about their lives. At the end, he held her as they talked about how fate brought them together.

"Tell me about your Tamaqua, Pennsylvania. Does it have a lot of people like Budapest? What about nice shops and cafés?"

Buck gave a slow grin and consoled, "No, darling, it has some small stores - hardware, clothing, a couple of diners but nothing like here and I imagine - not like Budapest either. However, they do have two movie houses.

"I live 2 miles outside of town where farms and quaint little houses dot the countryside. However, the people make this place special. They help their neighbors and never ask for anything in return. An unspoken bond of trust and fair play allows families to live without fear.

"Unlike Budapest, the area takes pleasure in simple things - tending vegetable gardens, raising farm animals, learning English and math in one-room schools or playing baseball on a Saturday afternoon."

Ilona tried to visualize such a place so different from the busy city where she grew up.

"My love, you know the Nazis continue to bomb the south of England including London at any time or place. I fear their destruction might find me someday. Will my time run out tomorrow, next week or next month? Oh Buck, this crazy war has turned me upside down. We only know each other for a short time but if the Allies win this war and we survive it, will you take me to Tamaqua? Far away from here. Somehow, I must seize every ounce of life before it flees from me."

He squeezed Ilona tight and nuzzled her face. "Darling, darling, take a deep breath. I can't make sense of it either. Every morning, I push aside all the what-ifs and maybes to face each day with my best effort.

"Ilona, the war brought you to me. I don't have time to think about how or why it happened but I won't let you go. When the war ends, I'll bring you home with me.

"You'll love my family. I have three brothers - a teen-age Edison with a working telegraph in the attic, a five year old, can ride a horse and full of the devil and the youngest...well, at a year old, he just smiles a lot. My parents come from the working class and judge people by their character, not someone's money or power."

*****

Ilona wanted the hot bath to last but soon after, with reluctance, they dried each other off. After she finished dressing, the phone rasped its irritating bell.

"Ilona here. Oh, hello Mary. Yes, I know we haven't talked since yesterday. Well...I've been busy. No. No. Entertaining an airman. Okay, I'll ask him."

She held her hand over the phone and asked, "Buck, since we don't have plans for this evening, do you mind having Christmas dinner with two very important people in my life? Mike and Mary Wright live just a short distance from here."

"My darling, sure I would love to join you and your friends this evening. Let's make it a night to remember."

"Mary, we'll be there. What time? Five?"

She looked at Buck.

He nodded okay.

"We'll see you then. Cheerio."

"Oh, oh, we can't go empty handed. Buck, please walk over to the Tetley canteen down the block and buy some tinned fruit. In the meantime, I'll run upstairs to pay off my black market source for some tinned vegetables. Mary will put them to good use in her mystery meat stew."

With presents in hand, she knocked on the couple's door. From the moment they arrived, Mary showered Ilona and Buck with hugs and kisses. Mike surprised everyone with a bottle of black market whiskey, adding to the merriment, but he made them promise not to ask questions of its source. They finished it off with a cake laced with raisins, cinnamon, cloves and a touch of orange. Mary boasted that her "war cake" is made without any butter or eggs but is as moist just the same.

Buck felt at home with the older couple and they in turn took an immediate liking to him. This festive gathering felt magical, like the world found peace and he returned to just being a bricklayer's son. His only reality - he loved the beautiful blonde woman sitting next to him.

As time passed, thoughts of future bombing missions and the uncertainty of it all, tried to seep into his conscious. However, he pushed all those unwanted details to the back of his mind.

Several hours later, feeling satisfied with good food, drink and conversation, they thanked Mary and Mike for a fantastic evening. They returned to Ilona's flat and listened to the latest BBC report on her wireless for any bombings in the area. An announcer reported events of a baby blitz occurring on the east of London with minimal damage. The RAF had already launched planes to counter the attack.

With a sigh of relief they tuned out the world and soon ended up in the bedroom. Their lust rampaged without limits, consuming each other, as if this Christmas night might be their last.

Several hours later, as Buck lay fast asleep, Ilona sat near a window overlooking the street. She took a draw from her cigarette, snapped off the ash and wondered where their relationship headed. It seemed so alien - thoughts of a permanent home, someone to love her and maybe even children.

The next morning, Buck shared coffee, many kisses and a tearful good-by. Ilona crashed into the reality of loving a military man. She will never know his missions or when he returns. Ilona cursed the war for being so unfair.

For weeks, his operations ran an unpredictable schedule. Ilona had no patience for news through normal channels so she developed contacts with several officers in 8th AAF headquarters. With their help, at least she had a chance to plan their time together.

Several weeks later, Ilona started feeling nauseated in the

mornings. She spent a lot of time crouched over the toilet, throwing up, or resting under some warm covers. Anxiety drove her to speak with Mary. She advised, "Dear, you need to see a doctor. You might be in a family way."

Pregnancy never entered her mind, but faced with the possibility, it raised a plethora of questions. How will Buck take this kind of news? If he walks away, can she support it? What happens if she no longer works? Will England deport her back to Hungary?

She debated whether or not to tell him. Mary suggested, "He has a right to know. After all, if you are carrying a child, he fathered it."

After settling with her own principles, Ilona reached a conclusion - tell him - but on her terms. "He'll return Monday, so I'll arrange to sing his favorite song - "I'll Be With You in Apple Blossom Time" - after the song, while he feels in a good mood, I'll tell him."

On her day of reckoning, Ilona wore the gown Buck loved; her emerald green that showed off her eyes best. As she began to sing, Ilona scanned the audience, but her lover's reserved chair sat empty. She remained calm and thought, "Buck will come, he promised."

Thirty minutes into her show, she began to sing - "I'll Be With You in Apple Blossom Time". Somewhere in the midst of her song Buck appeared in his favorite spot. It seemed so strange though, he wore brown leather flight gear instead of his uniform. She wanted to yell, "Don't move my darling, I want to tell you about our baby."

However, before she had a chance to finish the song, Buck waved an envelope and walked it to the bartender. Her lover blew a kiss and in an instant, disappeared from the room.

Ilona's stomach tied in knots, waiting for the finale to her song. She took an unscheduled break and hurried to the counter to retrieve Bucks letter.

*****

My Dearest Ilona,

I just received orders to ship out. Don't tell anyone, but I must leave England for a top secret assignment. I don't know how long, it might be weeks or months. We'll be out of touch for a while but when possible, I'll let you know what happens. I can’t wait until this war ends and we can be together.

Love,

Buck

P.S. I wrote my family about us and they can’t wait to meet you.

Chapter 22

Pregnant with God's Little Miracle

"God. Why do you hate me?" Ilona screamed to the ceiling, "First my family, then Uncle Gabe. The war needs Buck, but please - don't let him die.

"Oh Mary, the captain from headquarters hasn't received any word on his mission in weeks. I will go raging nuts if they don't find out soon.

"As for this innocent baby inside me, how will I care for it? How...God? And forget about abortion. I won't be one of those butchered women left to bleed out in some back alley.

"This unborn child belongs to us. I'll give birth and love it because if I lose Buck, the baby will be all I have."

Mary, who had been listening with patience, consoled, "Luv, ya know God doesn't give us anything unless he feels we can handle it. Besides, you always have Mike and me."

Ilona hugged Mary and wiped at tears. "I love you both. No

matter how bad I feel...you and Mike always give me hope.

"When Buck comes back, if he returns, I want to tell him. But I have so many doubts - at 19, how will he feel about having a child? I realize Buck's first obligation must be to serve his country and my pregnancy comes second. It will just complicate things for him."

"Ya don't have any easy choices," observed Mary, "confront him first off and maybe ya risk scaring Buck away.

"Or if ya don't tell him, it might buy some time to win his heart because yer in a family way."

Ilona contemplated, "Act as if nothing has happened? I continue singing and he goes on more missions? At least until I start showing? I...I can't just choose one over the other."

"Then child, you'll have to follow your conscience when the time comes."

"Mary, I've lived long enough to know when some experiences feel precious, valuable as gold.

"My husband, in Budapest, demanded sex often, but for all his miserable efforts, he failed to impregnate me; thank God.

"Buck and I have only been together a few times and now...now, I carry his child. I prefer to think this baby came from his goodness."

*****

Days plodded forward without word of Buck's whereabouts. Rumors about high B-17 losses filtered back to her through airmen she knew at the cabaret. However, Ilona tried not to think on it too much since the turmoil she harbored brought her to tears.

By late March, most of the harsh weather subsided and bright sunshine helped raise her spirits. Preparing for the evening's show, Ilona sat in her small cabaret, dressing room, listening to, “Don’t Sit Under The Apple Tree”, on the radio. She finished applying make-up, fluffed her hair and ran the words of some popular songs through her mind.

Without warning, the dressing room door swung open, framing several of the cigarette girls as they rushed in. Talking over each other, she struggled to understand them until her airman, hero and lover, followed them inside.

Rushing to his open arms, she cried, "Buck, oh Buck, I've missed you so.” Nuzzling her face to his chest, Ilona smelled the leathery aroma of his A-2 horsehide flight jacket. She missed the smell every time he embarked on a mission.

As the girls left, he rasped, "Darling, I love you," clinging to this delicate, feminine package.

"Hush, my love, just hold me. I feared the worst when I didn't hear from you."

"Yeah, headquarters kept a tight lid on this last mission, but I came back…for you.

"Hey…hey, Darling. Don't cry, did I say something wrong?"

Ilona sniffled, "No."

"For real…nothing? Something about you seems different. Your face looks a little puffy. Have you been getting enough sleep? Don't fret; I'll take extra good care of you.

"When this damn war is over, we can get on with our lives so stay strong for me, darling.

"I just heard some scuttlebutt about a new commander. Everybody says he can get the job done, lead us to victory plus all the officers respect him, not like Patton."

An elderly gentleman, dressed in tuxedo black, poked his head in the door, "Ilona, you're on in 5 minutes."

"Thanks, Jarvis."

"Okay, Buck. My band leader just gave me notice. I'll see you out front but first, kiss me for good luck."

As he sat in his favorite spot watching Ilona sing her heart out, he tried not to think of the work still to be done for his country. After so many weeks on mission, this night will be special.

*****

With white bed sheets strewn about and two naked bodies snuggled next to each other, the unwanted clanging of Ilona's alarm clock signaled the start of a new day.

Time slipped by too fast, but even a few hours together justified the travel it took to reach the one he loves. Buck never thought about the serious side of the word - love - before. Sure, he said it to his mom and maybe even to his baby brother just before he left for military training. But for a lover's love, it constituted a powerful word.

Ilona arose and prepared a fresh pot of coffee for Buck to keep him focused after the sleepless night of lovemaking. She even pressed his shirt and tie so he looked sharp for his commute back to base.

Buck and Ilona moved forward as lovers who cared for each other to the marrow. However, they also kept grave secrets, locked within their hearts, not to hurt, but to protect.

Orders from Buck's last briefing held top covert status. A mission so critical, any breach imposed a penalty of death by firing squad. He contained his anxiety so Ilona remembered their time together with fondness.

As for Ilona, she had also made a choice, just as serious. For right or wrong; she decided to spare Buck the burden of worry about an unborn child. At least for one more mission.

Chapter 23

Ilona's Choices

As time slogged forward and Ilona passed the first trimester of her pregnancy, nausea disappeared, appetite improved and the once tiny waistline began to expand. Because of her solid bone structure, the pregnancy remained undetectable to the public.

She continued to work, save and plan in secret, for the next stage of her life. With the Allied effort laying waste to Europe, and - V1 flying bombs - terrorizing everyone in England, she agonized every day over Buck's safety and the tiny life she carried.

Any free time found her huddled near the wireless, seeking Churchill's soothing voice. He reassured the people of Britain - despite every hardship, the Allies will win and Hitler's Nazi regime will pay for their atrocities.

On an early June morning, while at the kitchen table, she unfolded the "London News". Half awake, she expected the usual banter about the war. Standing up, eyes wide open, Ilona read the lead headline - INVASION IS ON - with full page articles detailing the large scale ship landings on French beachheads.

As she read further, additional information divulged eleven to twelve thousand aircraft entered the battle. Ilona wondered, "Has fate put you in harm's way, my darling? Damn, I feel so helpless."

*****

Without warning, she heard the front door open and a scurrying of feet across the wood floor.

"Luv…Luv, have ya heard? The allies attacked the Nazis at Normandy," Mary's voice snapped Ilona away from her desperate thoughts.

"Yes. And I'll wager Buck rode the first wave right into the thick of it. But I can't think about the invasion too much right now. Between feeling bloated, too hot or cold, craving odd foods and worry about the future, I have no energy left."

"Sit back and relax, Luv. Nothing you can do about this war except keep you and the baby healthy."

Mary's nurturing tendencies kept Ilona from neglecting her well-being during the pregnancy. "Luv, you need to start letting people know of your condition."

"What. Who cares about my pregnancy? I'll tell people when I feel like it."

"Child," Mary soothed, "you must do everything possible to keep up your strength. You know we have ration books to get our food."

"Of course."

"Well…the British government allows more rations for expectant mothers and children. You're entitled to it, you know."

"I had no idea. How does it work?"

"Take a look at your Ration Book."

Ilona clutched it from her purse.

"What jacket color do you see?"

"Tan, so what?"

"With your obvious pregnancy, you can request a green one. We'll find a midwife and have her write a note stating your condition to the proper government official.

"As an expectant mother, you need more milk and food. They allow two fresh eggs, not the powdered kind per week, a daily pint of milk, even orange juice and cod liver oil."

Ilona made a face, "Cod Liver Oil? Yuk. Why cod liver oil?"

"It maintains and builds your bones and the baby's too.

"The child can get more milk and food until it reaches five.

"Once you have the little one, we can plant a garden to grow our own vegetables. The exercise alone will help in your recovery and no more running to the market, except for meat."

"Oh Mary…Mary, I cannot see me working in a garden, even as a hobby. Just trying to stay alive in London consumes enough vigor, preparing for the show every night, much less the rationing and endless queuing for provisions.

"Food always seemed unimportant, a cup of coffee and a slice of heavy bread satisfied me. Now, I also have to eat for the baby."

"You can lean on me, Luv, I'll pick up your order for today and whenever you have a hard time of it.

"We use the same butcher and grocer. I'll just take your ration book along with me.

"Now…get dressed and step into the day. Tonight, give em a show worth remembering. Go on now; you have work to do."

Reaching out to squeeze Mary's hand, she offered, "I owe you so much. Maybe I'll survive this war after all."

Chapter 24

Prisoner of War

Sitting behind my dual Brownings, as the B-17 lifted off from England for a mission to Hanover, I had time to think about my future.

"I'll build a house further up the mountain, behind my father's wood-frame abode. Early every morning, between kisses, Ilona will pack my lunch pail with sandwiches of Kellner's bologna spread with spicy mustard on Eames soft white bread. Then I'll walk a short path to my father's place and chat for a moment with my family. Before long, Pop and I will head out to the latest construction site, a peaceful place where no one wants to shoot us."

Pulled out of my idle thoughts for a moment, I tended my routine check of ammunition, 50 caliber guns and communications. After crossing the channel, we flew east across Netherlands, following a course deep into North Germany.

During a lull in our flight, my stray thoughts turned to the current situation. "These missions keep coming, almost every day now; since the beginning of June. It's been nearly a month since I've seen Ilona. I wanted to tell her about the D Day mission over Normandy but she must know by now. Darling, we clobbered them all - Caen, LeHavre, Lisieux and Vire."

*****

Over the intercom, Spencer advised, "Buck, keep your eyes open; we just crossed Osnabrück. We have less than 100 kilometers traveling due west to Hanover. It may get rough, our agents reported at least 20 Messerschmitts based northwest of the city."

Looking out the rear canopy, I watched Osnabrück disappear over the horizon; yielding to green and brown of German farmland. My breathing increased and arms tensed in anticipation of those damn Nazi bastards in the skies above Hanover.

Without warning, Spencer yelled, "Okay - everybody - here they come."

Nazi aircraft swarmed us like an angry throng of yellow jackets. Like so many times before, my training and experience took over. Those Messerschmitts who chose to be aggressive soon found a hail of tracers ripping through their cockpit and engine cowling.

Over the next 30 minutes, I counted three Luftwaffe pilots who bailed out and four other aircraft, wafted heavy smoke, lost altitude and never returned. In the background, I heard our guy's Brownings raging almost non-stop.

As minutes ticked by, the assault subsided and we rushed to the flack-jacket cabinet. In our haste to don the vests, we heard the familiar explosive sounds of Nazi 88mm flak guns. Our B-17 entered the barrage of flak prepared for a bumpy ride but, as usual, only expected a few shrapnel holes.

I assumed my position in the tail and planned to sit out the next few minutes until our bombardier dropped several tons of explosives on Hanover-Misburg oil refinery.

*****

"What the hell!" I rasped, as the front of our plane lurched upward and the engines belched, sputtered and jerked about.

I yelled into the microphone, "Spencer, what happened? Spencer?...Spencer?"

By now the B-17 pitched and rolled about like a ship on rough seas. I stumbled toward the cockpit and found the waist gunners scrambling to get on their feet.

As the dysfunctional engines and odd whistling noise persisted, I shouted, "We need to get up front!"

We struggled toward the cockpit area only to find a large chunk of fuselage blown away. The bombardier and navigator lay on the floor like rag dolls, unmoving, covered in blood. Our radio operator moaned in pain and clutched at his chest.

While the waist gunners tended the radio operator, I pushed into the cockpit and found Spencer and his co-pilot riddled with shrapnel. Their seat belts held them upright as if they still held onto life.

I looked out the side windows and recoiled at the sight of two engines on fire and a third shrouded in smoke. From my pilot training back at Arner's Airport, I knew the autopilot struggled to hold our plane straight and level but only as long as the engines held speed and altitude. I figured we only had minutes to get out.

Joining the waist gunners in a hasty attempt to bind the radio operator's wound and strap him into a parachute, we carried him to the hatch door. We held the radio operator at the opening and then let him slip into the blue.

While we belted into our own chutes, the B-17 started to slow, losing altitude and entering a turn to the left. I knew the autopilot had disengaged. One by one we jumped free of the plane.

From my parachute, I watched the aircraft enter a steep spiral, nose dive, all the way to the ground. Upon impact, black smoke and fire billowed hundreds of feet into the air.

I grated, "Those poor bastards. They'll never see the end of this war."

Descending over wooded countryside just west side of Hanover, I hoped to reach the ground before those damn

Nazis had a chance to kill me in the air. From my position, I observed them racing toward the wreckage in Kübelwagens. Reconnaissance agents called them the equivalent of our jeeps.

I landed in dense forest, disposed of my chute and looked for the waist gunners. Setting down before me, I assumed they started to run west, toward the setting sun. Reaching Netherlands' border and the underground resistance near Enschede seemed our only hope.

*****

Using trees for cover gave me a sense of confidence in avoiding German soldiers. I estimated if my rate of travel covered twenty miles a day, I'll reach the Netherlands in about a week.

The first night, I found refuge near a stream. Although my sleep suffered, if they used blood hounds, I had a chance to hide my scent by staying in the water.

About noon the next day, woods gave way to cultivated fields and pastures. Although I avoided the roads, a few farmers saw me walking through their crops. I thought about wearing my shirt inside out or removing it, but if caught, the Nazi bastards might shoot me as a spy or worse - death by concentration camp.

By dark, I ventured upon a farm outside of Minden. It looked like any of the small homesteads however the barn lay several hundred feet behind the farm house, well away from German eyes and ears. Thoughts of a warm, comfortable sleep drove me inside. Careful not to rile any of the barn-yard animals, I curled up under a generous helping of hay and drifted off to sleep.

*****

As sunlight streamed through gaps in the walls, I heard the sound of boots, heavy boots, running toward my hiding place. Feeling numb, I realized the barn no longer provided sanctuary but cornered me like a rat.

"Amerikaner!...Amerikaner! We have you surrounded. How foolish, to think you can escape the German Wehrmacht. Do you understand? All citizens vow loyalty to mein Führer so these good farmers reported you at first sight. No Deutsch national will help you. Surrender now...or we will burn you out."

Taking a deep breath, I came to terms with my predicament. My escape plans will have to wait. I remembered Pop saying, "Do whatever it takes to survive." Those words gave me strength as I opened the barn door.

Squinting against the morning sun, I saw at least thirty soldiers armed with automatic weapons. In briefings, we called them grenadiers. In front of them stood a field officer, hands on hips, who sported green and gold collar insignias. Although my memory of their rank designations seemed rusty, I thought his green shoulder board with 2 gold diamonds made him a captain or hauptmann in German.

"All right Staff Sergeant...on your knees. Schnell (quick)! You have cost us enough time. We have yet to locate your slippery associates."

With sarcasm, I rasped, "You won't find them, with their experience, traveling 24 hours a day without sleep, my buddies have already reached the Netherlands underground."

Expecting some sort of response, I only saw the butt of a rifle for one brief second before it smashed into my head.

*****

I woke in what seemed like a holding room with several other airmen. I recognized them from our squad briefings though none of them ever flew with our crew.

"Oh man, my skull feels like hell."

"Yeah...well, you don't look so good either - between the goose-egg and dried blood. Butch McRay here, top notch tailgunner, also, Dave, our radio man and Charlie, waist gunner."

I nodded, "Good to meet you. Any idea how many planes we lost?"

"No, but the last I saw, our formation remained intact, dropping bombs dead-on the Hanover-Misburg oil refinery. We may be POWs now but you can believe our squad finished their mission. The Nazis can't take this win away from us."

Early next morning, two Waffen-SS soldiers, dressed in gray-green uniforms and armed with Luger pistols plus

MP38 submachine guns, trucked us for several hours to a large building.

Later on, we discovered their grim looking structure, located a short distance from Frankfurt, housed the German Intelligence Center, also called Dulag Luft.

Our two escorts, short on conversation, long on intimidation, marched us to a holding yard where we joined other captured airmen milling about. They all looked tired, nervous or devoid of any emotion.

Our spit and polish, well armed guards departed and left us with four overweight, disheveled soldiers carrying what our intelligence instructors called K98 standard issue rifles.

One at a time, I watched each airman enter the main building until my turn came. Escorted to an austere room with table and two chairs, I mentally prepared for a beating by some thugs or as I remember the term from high school German class - schlager.

I tried to hide my surprise when a short man in civilian suit, came into the space and shook my hand. He spoke English, asked about my well being and then commenced to discuss his childhood plus how he ended up as an interrogator.

Later in his discussion, he asked about my opinion of the war, how many missions I had flown, what position I filled with the crew, plus many more. Remembering my training back in England, I responded with name, rank and serial number. Without recrimination, he thanked me for the discussion and left.

Although I didn't know anything about interrogation strategy, I soon understood the concept of cooperation or punishment. The guards cast me into a small room with no windows plus single bed and let me stew for several days. On the third day, they brought me back to the same room, with the same interrogator. Again, I refused to divulge any information.

I think he lost interest after the fourth or fifth interrogation. However, the solitary confinement started to take its toll. I suffered from paranoia about the shadows in my room and long periods without sleep left me exhausted. I estimated at least three weeks had passed.

Without notice, they pulled me from my mental tormentor and along with other unfortunates, packed us, elbow to elbow, into a dusty boxcar. Scuttlebutt from the senior NCOs revealed our journey might end at a POW camp for NCOs run by the Luftwaffe called Stalag Luft IV near Gross Tychow, Pomerania.

We experienced a perplexing journey with many stops along the way. Some of our fellow POWs with railroad experience surmised our train ended up shunted onto a siding rail to make room for passing troop trains.

We consumed little food and not a drop of water. Those heartless bastards didn't even let us out to relieve ourselves, so we used Red Cross cartons. A nauseating stench soon overwhelmed our boxcar in the July heat while an army of flies invaded the waste.

Suffering hunger, thirst and weakness, at the end of a long and dreary train ride, over 500 of us stumbled out of our moving prisons. They didn't waste any time lining us up and double timing about a mile to the front of a depressing camp, filled with small huts.

I listened to Germans yammering back and forth for several minutes. Visions of my high school German class and all the repetition came back to me as I tried to translate their conversation. Most of it came so fast, I couldn’t understand. However, their last sentence, "Fahren sie in den Suden Verbindung," made sense. They aimed to take us to a south compound.

Wooden gates, covered in barbed-wire, opened and then closed behind us. Cold realization set in, this must be the end for me - a POW camp. As we walked further, barracks after barracks slid by, all looking like each other - bland and simple in construction.

The outer walls of the compound seemed at least 8 feet tall and consisted of rough-cut wooden posts with inhumane fence wire pulled tight around the perimeter. The kind of wire meant to shred a person bloody if he tried to negotiate those man-made thorns.

Without warning, several of the guards rasped, "Stehen bleiben".I understood not only the hostile tone, but their words, demanding we stop. I also noticed they appeared to be low-level soldiers – lacking the calm demeanor of someone in authority.

For the first time, I smelled fear in the air and saw it in the eyes of my fellow POWs. I nodded at those around me, trying to show we faced this together. Even though strangers, we all wore the uniform of the 8th.

"Schnell, Schnell, Antreten!" yelled the guards. After some shouting and pointing, we figured they wanted us to line up in military fashion. We assumed the position of a platoon but without any purpose, except to survive.

We waited for several minutes before a Kübelwagens pulled up to the area. A rugged looking but elderly SS officer struggled out of the vehicle and swaggered toward us. He carried a clip board under his arm and wore the Iron Cross, Germany's medal for valor, around his neck. The other officer, appearing very young, carried his arm in a sling and followed several paces behind.

The young officer assumed a formal position, clicked his heels together, arms held close to his side and yelled, "Aufmerksamkeit" (attention)! Although I felt like punching the arrogant bastard, I came to attention and stared straight ahead.

The senior Nazi seemed focused on his clipboard for a moment then eyed us over, "Guten Tag, (good day) prisoners. You are now a guest of the Reich and subject to articles of the Geneva Convention.

"I feel generous today, so on this special occasion, you will have the privilege of understanding my philosophy about the clash between Germany and the Allies. America will soon capitulate, just like Poland. I led one of the first assaults in 1939. Our Blitzkrieg crushed their western defenses and drove them like sheep to the southeast. We will do it again on your soil.

"Unfortunately, I will no longer lead my men into battle. I've served the fatherland since my youth and seen my share of war. The Führer feels my place…belongs here.

"So...we must make the best of it. Be warned, the war no long exists, for you. Submit to the rules of this camp and your stay will be comfortable. If not…trouble-makers, saboteurs and those trying to escape will suffer harsh punishment."

*****

Converting from airman to prisoner-of-war dulled my sense of purpose. How can I serve the 8th as a tailgunner while cooped up in this mediocre POW complex? I also feel offended being called prisoner 8008 or, acht null null acht, by the guards.

"So many unanswered questions. What the hell happened to our waist gunners? I hope they made it all the way back to England. And the flak - squadron protocol always kept us just above the 88mm anti-aircraft range. A fluke or maybe the Nazis experimented with more powerful cannon?"

"Hey Buck, yer talking to yerself again. Stop thinkin about what happened. Yer here now, it ain't the Ritz but at least ya have a roof over yer head and lots of buddies in the same boat."

"Sure Brooklyn," PFC Paul Krauser - prisoner 8109, a kid from Brooklyn and radio operator, "Thanks for the uplifting sermon. I realize your trip to this hellhole took the same path as mine yet you just take it in stride. Well, no more grousing about how my life turned out. What delicious morsels will we consume for dinner?"

"Pheasant under glass, potatoes au jour, apple pie a la mode, and a tanker of ice cold beer, Special Sergeant Buck Remke, sir."

"Sure, smart ass. By the way, what happened to our dinner server?"

"You mean the lucky guy who stands in line outside the kitchen, fetches our slop bucket, and brings us those dainty portions? Of course, he'll be careful not to over-feed us so we don't lose our girlish figures."

"Brooklyn, your warped sense of humor does not help my growling stomach. However, I hope they stop making sauerkraut soup since their last batch turned my stomach. Remember, we had to sneak a bucket full to the latrine and dump it."

"The potato soup seemed okay until they added kohlrabi. My bunkmate, Benny, told me they feed kohlrabi to their cows back home in Iowa. Those bovines have my sympathy. At least the barley cereal tasted good, it seems to sit well in my stomach."

"And who can forget the black bread and tar colored liquid they pass off as java. The cooks call it - ersatz coffee. They pulled a fast one with the fancy name since it just means replacement coffee. I hear the cooks use acorns to give it a brown color."

"But at least when they serve it hot, you can almost imagine being there, smelling the aroma while it perks."

"Hey, Buck, you failed to mention the big event when we sit around watching the food server divide our loaf of black bread into eight equal pieces. He cuts it with precision, like a surgeon."

"The damn bread has no yeast so it comes out hard and dense. But in spite of its unpleasant texture and taste, it holds you for a while. I sometimes store a piece in my shirt pocket. It helps hold off the hunger when they serve spoiled food or if we make a break for it."

"Buck?...Buck? You hear it? Sounds like a lot of planes headed somewhere close by."

"God damn, Brooklyn, they just sounded the air raid! Hit the deck!

"Flat on the floor," I yelled, "Bomb those bastards straight to hell!"

*****

Over three months of my life had passed, serving no useful purpose, and a hard chill of approaching winter permeated the air. We remained imprisoned in the camp and work on escape plans had been curtailed.

After the SS ignored the Geneva Convention and shot 50 POWs for trying to escape from Sagan, our government no longer considered it a duty to break out of confinement.

We hid the plans of various escape routes inside a latrine wall. Although our choices seemed bleak, we had selected to travel by night to Gdansk and board a ship to one of the Nordic countries. The city lay in turmoil from Soviet bombings and a massive German civilian exodus. Our chances of infiltrating the city seemed better than negotiating our way west to Germany or south through Poland.

The commandant increased sentries around the perimeter including trigger-happy guards in the towers. During an assembly, he declared, "All POWs caught trying to escape will be shot without warning."

To keep from going crazy, I started accumulating information about the camp. At first I questioned other POWs and later - approached guards. There appeared to be five compounds or as the Germans call them - lagers. They referred to each lager by letter - lager A to lager E. The Waffen SS maintained responsibility of 40 POW huts and each hut contained 200 men. As for me and my buddies, we called lager A, our temporary home.

*****

Sgt Eddie Pulski, 8030, from Pittsburgh, PA, sacked out in the lower bunk, radio operator for a B-17G. During his tenth mission, a JU 88 twin-engine fighter shot him down over

Aalborg, Denmark. Eddie marked time from all the way back to February.

He seemed about 19. Hell, all of them looked so young. But my buddies, losing enough of their body weight to look like skeletons, shocked me to the core. I felt grateful the hut had no mirrors.

Late one evening, about 6 of us sat around a small table playing poker. After watching Eddie struggle through several hands, I grabbed his arm and asked, "Hey, why can't you stop shivering?"

"Huh, how the hell do I know, Buck? Every day gets colder and this lousy hut has no heat. I don't have any baby fat or hot blooded babes to keep me warm. And those Nazi bastards - they only give us worn British clothes and a couple of thin blankets."

"Yeah Eddie, I'll bet our Red Cross parcels, the ones we never received, have plenty of fresh uniforms and blankets. At least our compound received one thick blanket each from Uncle Sam back in September. I've developed quite an attachment to it."

"It helps, but I swear to God, Buck, the scratchy German one, made of horse hair, drives me crazy. When it rubs against my skin, I can't sleep at night."

"I gave up trying to be comfortable in bed right after we arrived here. Eddie, you can believe the Nazis gave us those miserable blankets on purpose. They don't want us to get a good night's rest. Sleep in your clothes. They may get wrinkled and smell like hell but you'll have more energy to fight off the cold.

"I have another good reason for staying dressed. Remember in August when they made an emergency inspection during the middle of the night. We had to leave our bunks and line up in the assembly yard wearing just our underwear? Right then, I made the decision, military standards of dress and hygiene mean nothing here. The ability to adapt and a mind set to survive this hell get me through the day."

"Ya know, Buck, when I complain about our conditions to Hauser, our talkative German sergeant, he tells me to feel lucky because at least we have burlap mattresses filled with wood shavings. Some of the other kriegies (POW's call themselves this) sleep on a filthy floor.

"But it gets worse. With winter coming, he says the temperatures sink below freezing around December and stay there until early March. Damn it, Buck, look at the compound just north of us, it doesn't even have a chimney."

*****

PFC Benny Wilson, 8025, waist gunner, a farm kid from Iowa, slept in the cot under me. He lied about his age to enlist, which meant in the eyes of the 8th, the kid didn't even qualify for combat duty. I must admit, for seventeen, he stood tall and looked massive.

I came to understand why the 8th had age limits. Although

he hid it well, late at night, I heard Benny crying but didn't think any less of him. He had good reason to be afraid. The guards shot POWs just for wandering around outside at the wrong time. And even though the camp didn't seem to have any sophisticated forms of torture, beatings and harassment occurred every day.

During our long hours of boredom, Benny complained about the Geneva Convention. "These German bastards don't honor the damn agreement. The Red Cross comes in to inspect our quarters, Nazis force us to spruce it up in advance and even if we protest in person, nothing ever changes.

"And what happened to our packages with meat, tinned fruit, chocolate bars and cigs? When we do get any provisions, the Nazis puncture the containers so we have to eat them right away. They know we'll hoard them and try to escape.

"But if you want to know the most evil insult to our existence just look at this sour black bread they feed us. Everyone swears it contains sawdust and whatever else they sweep up from the floors. No wonder my gut feels like hell all the time."

"Don't let them win, Benny. Think about your parents. You need to make it home and help them on the farm. My biggest gripe, I haven't had a shower or change of clothing in months. Every day, I shake the lice out of my clothing and wipe them off my body from head to toe. It drives me crazy."

Dwelling on the things I had no power to change, grew intolerable. To quell those haunting thoughts, I called across the day room, "Hey, Brooklyn, what kind of entertainment do you have lined up for this evening?"

"Well...press your tuxedo and shine some dancing shoes, we'll go raise hell at the Stork Club."

"Smart Ass."

"Okay, Buck, how about I entertain you with a German lesson? Can't hurt to know what these goons say about us. Heh, heh, reminds me - I can't believe these guards still think goon means German-Officer-Or-Noncom. I don't want to be here when they find out it represents a hairy, low IQ runt.

"Anyway, my folks came over on the boat from Germany in 1921 and my mom birthed me at the Norwegian Hospital in Brooklyn a short time later. They love America and raised all their kids the same.

"Of course, they never thought their oldest son might end up in a Nazi prison camp. It breaks their hearts.

"Mom scrubbed floors and dad worked on the docks until they saved enough money to open a German butcher shop. The bologna just melted in your mouth. A dab of horseradish, mustard and some good rye bread - what heaven."

Buck chimed in, "Forget the German lesson, I'll end up knowing just enough to get into trouble. We need to keep you up front - pushing, probing and befriending these goons for information about everything and anything."

Without warning, the only door, at the far end of our hut opened, letting in cold air and two guards.

"Oh, oh, here comes Hauser, our ferret or maybe - guardian angel? Okay Buck, goon up. Stand at attention."

"Geez, Brooklyn, he wants the war to end just like us. In my opinion, I don't think he cares who wins, long as he can go home to his family."

"Sure, but don’t turn your back. Just because he speaks English, doesn’t make him our friend."

"I don't disagree with you. Maybe he does have a plot to gain our trust and then run to the commandant with information. Look, I'll handle him if you start working on the other guard who only speaks German. Try to find out about the war, this camp, POWs, anything."

"Okay, Buck, I'll give it a try. No guarantees though."

I waited until Hauser walked to my end of the hut and nodded to join me at a table.

As we sat across from each other, I whispered, "What scuttlebutt do you have for me?"

"For two cigarettes, I tell you, 8008."

I reached into my shirt pocket and slipped them under the table. "Okay, Hauser, enjoy the last of my cigs. Now, what happened over the last week?"

"We received more prisoners from another Stalag."

"Will there be some pretty Air Force nurses?"

"You wish for the impossible. Only British RAF airmen."

"Where will you put them all?"

"Our Kommandant says the D & E lagers. We ran out of beds so they sleep on the floor for now."

"Officers and NCOs?"

"Nein, the Officers go to another Stalag Luft. Geneva Agreement, remember 8008? "Officers and NCOs are separated, but you already know this."

Hauser looked around and then whispered, "Do not test me. If this compound commits any war crime against Kriegies I will report it to you."

"Okay. Okay. Fair enough. One last thing, our guys gripe all the time about those Red Cross packages? We haven't had a shipment in weeks."

"Enough questions 8008, or word will get to the Kommandant, we fraternize."

Before he stood up, I looked him in the eyes and stated, "Danke, Hauser."

He retorted, "Sie sind willkommen (you are welcome)," and left our hut with the other guard.

I looked across the room at Brooklyn. He shook his head and shrugged his shoulders. I vowed not to let Brooklyn's German skills go to waste. I'll keep pushing him until we can bribe another guard for information. Just in case something happens to Hauser.

As I headed back to the day room, Eddie waved his arm and yelled, "Yo Buck, how about some poker?"

"Geez, no can do. I traded the last of my cigarettes to Hauser. Anyway, how do you feel today?"

"Like crap, the gourmet food from this first-class kitchen gives me the runs. I've been gnawing on charcoal from the wood stove. A kriegie from the other hut says it helps to clear up dysentery."

"Well...I have a feeling we'll all get it before long. By the way, you track the mail deliveries. Did it come today? We still get mail on Tuesdays. Right?"

"Damned if I know, Buck. I haven't heard a peep from the commandant's office. Since the war interferes with mail transit, it takes a month or two for an answer. I sent my quota of two letters and four postcards a few weeks ago."

"You sent all six at the same time?"

"Sure, this way, my mom will get at least one of them. She must be sick with worry by now. You see, my dad passed-on soon after I enlisted and she has no one else.

"Life already kicked her in the gut when my two older

brothers died in a friggin mine accident. Sure, I enlisted for the war effort, but also to stay out of those damn West Pennsylvania coal mines. If I survive this, I'll take my mom far away from Pittsburgh.

"Say Buck, what about the Hungarian singer? You know - the pretty blonde you told me about, the one in London who stole your heart."

"I sent her most of the letters and postcards and they all came back, stamped with red ink - no one at this address. I can't believe she left without letting me know. I even gave her my folks address in Pennsylvania just in case anything happens to me."

"Buck, some of our new kriegies said the Nazis have been launching a constant barrage of V1 rockets into London since mid-June. Maybe she moved or the Army evacuated her?"

"My God Eddie. She lives in the heart of London. How can I protect her while rotting away in this Nazi quagmire?"

"Calm down, Buck. You can help her best by staying alive and keeping your head. Think it through...does she have a next of kin or some friends?"

"Ilona has no living family, but she loves this elderly couple They live near Essex Road, in Islington; not too far, a short tube ride from her flat. Soon as I get out of here, I'll find them. Thanks for keeping me from going off the deep end."

*****

I tried my best to sleep at night in spite of the predictable screaming episodes from Benny, at least a couple of times per week.

"Benny! Cut it out. You had a bad dream again."

"Oh God, oh God, please get me out of here!"

"Take it easy, kid. No one wants to hurt you."

He jumped out of bed, pacing back and forth like a caged animal.

"I can't sleep without dreaming of our wing and mid-section being shredded by flak. I didn't even recognize my buddy on the other waist gun. Part of his face and shoulder had been ripped apart. Our radio operator lay in a pool of blood, staring up at me until I felt the life drain from his body. Those damn Nazi butchers, I'd kill them all if I had the strength."

"C'mon kid, settle down. Tell me how it all happened. Get it off your chest, maybe then you can have some peace."

"Aw right, ok," he exhaled, as Benny started to recount the events bringing him here. "I joined the 8th in November of '42 and trained as a waist gunner on B-17s. Ya know, the two waist gunners have to stand. We make a bigger target because the rest of the crew can sit or kneel. Anyway, they sent me overseas as part of the European Theatre Operations in '43.

"Well, early one morning, we started this bombing mission

over Germany. Who knew my twenty third operation turned out to be jinxed? I'll never get a chance to complete the final two. Damn, just a few more and home.

"Anti-Aircraft fire shot us up real bad and the remaining crew parachuted near a small village. I landed further from the town but watched civilians, acting like crazed vigilantes. They beat and hanged our co-pilot on the spot.

"Several of our crew managed to slip away and we almost made it to Minden before the Wehrmacht captured us. I felt impressed when a German lieutenant said they activated several thousand volunteers just to find us.

"They trucked the remnants of our team to Dulag Luft and started the grilling process. Interrogators first session included the obvious declaration - Vas Du Das Krieg Est Uber which they made a point of translating to English – "For You the War is Over".

"I didn't know what to expect when they herded us like sheep to the center. We had all received training about only divulging - name, rank and serial number. But the anxiety set my heart to racing."

Though we only had a few hours until sun-up, I urged Benny to continue.

"Well, this German big shot tried to be my friend. He looked all spit and polish and spoke pretty good English, for a Jerry, if ya know what I mean."

"Yeah, Benny. We all had our turn with interrogators and

their head games."

"He told me to fill out the Red Cross Form. It had questions about birth place, parents' names and unit assignment. When I hesitated, they threatened not to notify my folks about being captured."

"So what happened next?"

"I stuck to name, rank and serial number."

"You did good, because their form, whether called Red Cross or not, gives them vital information about our military operations."

"Well...the sour pusses threw me in solitary, a little six by eight cell. The only lighting came from a hallway, making it dark and scary. Also, the room had no toilet so I depended on the guard for my latrine breaks. However, he always seemed annoyed so I kept them to a minimum.

"Next day, - Major Spit n Polish - pushed me again to fill out their form. But this time he said it represented a minor formality. He told me when the 8th issued my serial number and at which training facility. He also told me stuff about my air force unit."

"Don't worry about it; they have tactics to secure a limited amount of information without our help."

“When the major saw my ID photo, he described our air base. How does he access this type of inside knowledge?"

"Look where the mess sergeant stamps your meal ticket. It

has a unique design. Once the major identified your mess sergeant, they had the base." You did not divulge any confidential information, kid. Also, did anyone bring photographic equipment aboard?"

"Sure, some of us did. I promised my sister I would take pictures for the nephew."

"Did they confiscate the camera from you?"

"Yeah. Hell, who thought a lousy Kodak, Brownie commanded so much attention."

"If you took pictures of the base or mission and they salvaged the film, intelligence will extract any usable information from every frame."

"Holy cow, how do you know about all this, Buck?"

"Technical Sgt Kelly, our MOC, better known as Man of Confidence. He filled me in; it seems that Sgt. Wynisky, the guy in the bunk across the hut experienced the same situation. The MOC knew about these things from the scuttlebutt that goes around. Don't worry, you didn't mean any harm."

"So...I refused to fill out the form and they took my camera. My punishment...several more days of solitary. I think they assigned a big goon to intimidate me. He must have weighed 300 pounds at least, big neck, bad teeth, and spit as he yells. The goon spoke no English but I felt him on the verge of breaking my neck several times."

"Damn Benny. Sounds like they went out of their way to give you grief."

"Yeah. I just closed my eyes and thought about family back on the farm. Otherwise, I might have gone crazy.

"When the interrogators gave up on me, about 30 SS guards marched a batch of us onto cattle cars. They crammed every POW in so tight, we all had to stand. During a stop for water, the guards allowed everyone to relieve ourselves by the tracks. Otherwise our only option remained standing up. We felt like animals.

"The train chugged into a crude rail station where the goons unloaded our tired group and walked us to Stalag VI. Boy, it felt like a country club compared to this place. We had a competent MOC and the Germans treated POWs straight-up. They kept us in clean clothes, running water and tolerable food.

"We received frequent Red Cross Parcels and shared them with other POWs. With the first arrival, one of the men ate his SPAM, chocolate bars and fruit at one setting. He had the heaves and runs for two days. But, like all good things, our stay came to an end seven months later."

"Benny, it flabbergasts me. How in the world did you end up here?"

"Although rumors flourished about some high level power struggle with Himmler, the commandant said complications with the International Red Cross and a threat of Russian troops advancing to the west forced closing of our camp in

July. I heard the SS transported Allied officers to Luft 1 and 3.

"On the first leg of our evacuation, the Nazis shipped over one thousand American airmen on a captured Russian ship. After docking at port, they divided us into small groups, removed our shoes and socks to prevent any escape and loaded each unit onto a train. After five days we arrived at Kiefheide Station.

"Placing our feet on solid ground and breathing fresh air didn't prepare us for this crazy, red faced captain, waving his arms and yelling “Laufen”. Most of us soon found out it meant run. They forced us to jog about three miles to the camp prodded by bayonets and attack dogs. Those more able bodied airmen helped the weakest keep up.

"The locals, including children, yelled, spit and tossed stones. They called us Luftgangsters, which one of our guys interpreted as terror fliers. It implies we murder women and children."

"Well, you survived and made it here, Benny. Not everyone has the grit to carry on. What about Red Cross packages? Did you bring any along?"

"Naw. When we started on the journey, the SS made us leave all of them behind. They promised to freight them to this camp but it never happened. I heard the Brits got theirs. I'll bet a lot of Nazis smacked their chops on Spam and smoked our Lucky Strikes. These bastards have no sense of integrity; they lie and indulge in greed or violence on a whim."

"Let it go Benny, don't let them get to you."

*****

"Get down!" I screamed, as explosions rocked the hut, several windows shattered and dust sifted through the air. Although I knew the shrill siren screamed around me, my hearing sounded muffled like a bad speaker on Pop's Philco radio.

Several minutes later, after the blitz subsided, Benny exclaimed, "God damn, another air raid! The tenth one today, they keep getting closer."

"I know kid, but we have to keep going - through the next hour, the next day, the next month. Remember this, next time you hit the dirt - above all else, stay alive for your family and anyone you ever cared about.

"The Allies will come, believe it. And when the day comes, we will spit in the eye of, der Kommandant, and walk out of here as free men."

*****

The ranking sergeant bellowed, "Roll Call!"

I grouched, "Geez, after all the commotion last night, just gives me a few more minutes. It can't be morning yet."

"Staff Sergeant Remke, You know the rules. Up and at em. Fall in men. Move it."

Looking out the window, I observed, "You see the cold and

rain out there. I hate it."

"Listen, Commandant Kessler loves to punish us. Most of all, he has it in for Technical Sergeant Kelly, our Camp Leader."

"Why?" I inquired.

"He thinks Kelly smuggled a radio into the barracks."

"I assume Kessler didn't find one?"

"No, Buck, he disassembles it after the BBC newscast. But Kessler has ways of coercing the prisoners. He threatened to withhold food and recreation to the entire A Lager if he finds it. Let's not give him a reason to tear up the barracks and throw our food stash onto this filthy floor."

"Ok, you win, roll call coming up."

"Let's get this count right, men, so we can wrap it up in fifteen minutes instead of three hours like yesterday. Damn this cold weather."

Chapter 25

Coping

She had even more in common with mentor, cabaret singer and new mother - Maria. Her mentor recommended a midwife to visit and check on the pregnancy. Although early in her child carrying, the midwife explained proper diet and exercise.

She didn't discuss concerns about the small pelvic proportions as plenty of time existed to suggest an obstetrician in case of a Caesarean-section. With luck, as the baby grew and gained weight, her pelvis will expand resulting in a successful normal delivery.

Performing a cabaret show every night, Ilona had to pay close attention to her tummy as it expanded. When the time came, Ilona decided to tell Niles about the latest chapter in her life, but she wondered about his reaction.

In her flat, she rocked in a new chair, bought for lulling the anticipated baby to sleep. Reaching for the phone, she dialed her manager's number. "Hello Niles, Ilona here. I need a favor. Can we talk today, in your office? Good."

Ilona went about her day. However, instead of rehearsing new songs, she reviewed her savings. She questioned, "How long after the baby's birth can I survive without resuming work. Will Buck return and share his future with me and the baby?"

Looking into a long mirror at her figure, she no longer seemed undernourished. Mary always teased her about skimping on food. For years, she used to fantasize about displaying ample breasts and hips. Her tiny waistline increased but given everything else happening to her body, it didn't matter.

She pondered, "Will I regain my figure after the baby comes? Can I give my child the attention it needs after I go back to work?"

Ilona took a minute to think back on her own life. She recalled a carefree childhood, playing in the park with István while their parents watched from a public bench, stealing a discrete kiss every now and then, and grandma Sára making beigli and strudel for the holidays. "What memories will I give to my child?"

A loud knock on the door brought her back to reality. Mary dropped by and reminded her to drink the daily ration of milk and keep an appointment with her manager, Niles.

*****

Later in the afternoon, Ilona stood in front of Niles' desk looking like a disobedient schoolgirl.

"No, Ilona, first Maria and now you. I can't lose my best singer. Who did this to you? I'll knock his block off."

"Niles, please, you already met the father - Buck Remke. He has always been a gentleman and we love each other."

"The bloody Yank tailgunner? Well...if he doesn't treat you right, I'll...I'll...report him to President Roosevelt. As for you, let's try to figure out how much time before the baby starts showing. The cabaret will carry you, long as possible. Ilona, on a personal note, when the time comes for your delivery, I want to know if you need anything, hear me - anything."

*****

During quiet moments in the flat, Ilona held her ear to the wireless, trying to hear news about the landing of the Allied combat troops along the Northern Coast of France. She listened intently to the voice of Prime Minister, Winston Churchill announcing that there was heavy bombardment by the planes from all Allied Air Forces and imagined Buck up there doing his job. After each broadcast, she uttered, "Go get um Buck." Later on she caught snatches of the voice of the Supreme Commander of the Allied Expeditionary Force, General Dwight D. Eisenhower. He addressed the people of Western Europe and informed them of the invasion.

And at the end of most long days, Ilona crawled into bed listening to the sounds of bombing, in the south of London. Even daylight refused to offer safety, as air raid sirens screamed, she hobbled from her small flat to the overcrowded, foul smelling bomb shelter.

She moved with caution since her swollen body made for unsteady feet. The once slim, sculptured ankles mushroomed to almost twice their size. The inflated stubs forced her to lie down often. "Too much salt," warned the midwife at her last visit.

"I can't control it," retorted the soon-to-be mother, "salt hides in everything - bacon, sausage, even powdered eggs. I qualify for eggs, straight from the hen, but so often the grocer runs out of them. And I may be crazy but those taste salty too."

The mid-wife instructed, "Just stay off your feet, as much as you can. Swelling, called edema can be dangerous for you and the unborn baby. I am concerned that your blood pressure is higher than normal; I'll come back in a few days to check on you."

Shocked at the midwife's stern assessment, Ilona responded, "I promise, feet up, at every chance."

As the delivery date approached, she felt anxious about her next stage of life. Questions churned over and over in her mind.

"After the baby's birth, will I end up a single mother, struggling to raise my child alone, dependant on the government?

"Oh my precious Buck, please return and take us in your

arms. Fly me and the baby to your home in Pennsylvania where we'll be happy forever.

"Dear God, please let me hear from him. Why doesn't the 8th Command respond to my inquiries? I don't even want to consider him missing or killed in action."

With this thought, Ilona wept as she faced a grim reality - the war ripped away every shred of comfort. Except for Mike and Mary plus a few friends, she faced the world alone.

*****

With her stomach protruding beyond the limits of acceptance, she bid a heart wrenching but temporary goodbye to the cabaret. She concentrated on keeping the baby healthy and following her mid-wife's medical advice.

As Ilona approached the ninth month, she started to feel cramps in her lower back, which evolved into a stabbing ache, then stopped flat. She took a deep breath, "Ouch, I wonder if that was a labor pain!" Just as abrupt, an avalanche of hurt overwhelmed her and warm, wet fluid saturated her nightgown.

She struggled to slide out of bed and reach the phone on her night stand. Ilona grated, "Mary, I just leaked water all over my bed and feel lousy. I think the baby wants out."

Soon after, Mary arrived and wiped her forehead with a wet cloth. "Child, you broke water for sure and are in labor. We best get you to the hospital straight away. Pack some things and I'll get the midwife. Also, Mike's friend has a car. Don't worry Luv, everything will be fine."

Bouncing through the debris strewn thoroughfares of London, the pains grew worse and came closer together. Ilona moaned, "Little baby, I can't wait to meet you and get rid of this belly… and this…this…pain."

When they arrived at the maternity unit outside of the city, Mary helped her out of the car and wheeled her to admitting. A pleasant nurse helped her get settled in bed and the midwife arrived within the hour for a pre-delivery examination.

The mid-wife advised, "Try to relax, Ilona, you need a few more centimeters of dilation. It will take a while, so try to control your breathing.

"I have four other expectant mothers at this facility. I picked this remote maternity unit so no one will have a bad time of it because of buzz bombs exploding over their heads.

"Now, I have a frank but necessary question to ask. As a single mother, do you still plan to keep this baby?

"I work with the National Children's Adoption Association. If you choose, they can make arrangements, any time. Even though most indigenous couples want British babies, many good families look for European children. Should you choose not to keep the baby, I can promise it a good home."

"I know you mean well nurse. But nothing...nothing will keep this baby from me. Right now, his father defends

England somewhere over the skies of Germany. I will not deny my child's birthright, no matter the cost to me."

*****

"I can't stand it, please…please…give me something," Ilona cried, "I've been in labor well over twenty four hours, please bring the doctor. Cut it out of me now. Oh God...oh God, the pain doesn't stop."

"Dear child, calm down, take deep breaths. Another shot of Morphine is coming for you straight away. I will give you my best effort but most of our doctors volunteered for the military. So women closest to delivery have priority. Besides, I now have five deliveries scheduled."

Ilona tried to roll on her side to face the mid-wife, "What? I thought you only had four patients. How soon do I come up for delivery?"

"Birthing doesn't stop because of the war. Three, before you, already delivered healthy babies, and now, four more checked in today. Don't worry, you will be scheduled soon."

"No. You've got to understand me, it doesn't feel right inside and I need to throw up. Nurse, no matter what, don't lose my baby - Buck's baby."

Examining her patient, the midwife noticed a trickling of blood onto the bedclothes. She felt the tenseness of Ilona's abdomen, "Ow," shouted Ilona, "it hurts." Continuing the examination, she listened to the fetal heart sounds. Ilona's concern rang true - they were very weak and the baby was in distress.

She feared the placenta had separated from the wall of her uterus. The mid-wife also knew, if this occurred, the patient might hemorrhage, resulting in the fetus deprived of its oxygen supply. Since this complication was way beyond the skills and training of a midwife, she wasted no time finding the doctor to examine her.

Locating the bone weary doctor before he headed down the hall to another patient, the mid-wife explained, "Doctor, I have a most urgent delivery. My patient has been in labor for well over twenty four hours. Her fetal heart sounds are weak and irregular; I think we may lose her. Within the last hour, she noted vaginal bleeding and suffers intolerable pain. Her blood pressure is severely elevated, and I think her small pelvis will not allow the baby's head to engage."

"Okay, okay let's see your patient, but hear my frustration young lady. I've inherited a mad house with more patients than any one doctor can handle.

"Compound this with the buzz bombs hitting closer every week - buzz bombs, doodlebugs, V1's- whatever they call the bloody bastards. We've been lucky so far, but one day, those Jerrys will blow the bloody roof off. And I refuse to scurry inside one of those foul smelling shelters.

"Too many specialists now serve on the front. Even though my practice has been obstetrics for the last 15 years, I just removed an appendix. The patient almost died, since a routine procedure took me twice as long."

The doctor examined Ilona, checked her vitals and reassessed the fetal heart sounds. He reflected, "I concur, we have a serious situation; her blood pressure rests in dangerous territory; the fetal heart is weak; looks like a premature placental separation. I'll have to remove the baby from her surgically and she will need blood. We don't have much time, let's hope and pray she makes it."

After hours of miraculous life saving efforts, a drowsy Ilona awoke from the anesthesia feeling nauseated, painful and weak. She looked up at the ward sister and asked, "My baby, did it survive?"

"Yes and you'll find him an impatient and hungry little bloke who let us know he wants his mum."

"A boy? I had a baby boy?"

"A beautiful baby boy. Do you feel strong enough to nurse him?"

"I...I don't know; I can hardly move."

"I'll hold his bottom side while you nurse him," piped Mary who had been parked in the hallway, "We came up when your mid-wife phoned about the surgery. Don't worry Luv, Mike and I will help."

The new mother, in spite of all her pain, seemed to perk up after holding the precious newborn to her breast. Ilona's boy suckled with voracious fervor as she soothed, "Everything will be all right my little fellow; I've got you now."

*****

Throughout the day, as if to remind Ilona - nothing had changed outside – buzz bombs exploded off in the distance, maybe thirty kilometers away. She ignored them, thinking, "I'll survive this war for my baby and when Buck comes back to us."

A determined new mother, despite her weakened condition, cared for little István, who she named after her brother. She also felt grateful - without the support of Mary and Mike, her baby might have been taken. In their joy, baby István had already received the pet name of Pip.

Little Pip, in spite of his arduous beginning, seemed to thrive. He responded with enthusiasm to his own personal audience of Ilona, Mary and Mike. Except for sleeping, his tiny body appeared to be attached to one of their willing laps. The team of this loving couple afforded Ilona valuable sleep time which her poor dilapidated body required.

"Pip, darling, look who came to see you today - Mary and Mike," Ilona uttered to her precious bundle.

She already saw familiar traces of her family's features in his little face. "I think you will be a green-eyed blonde like your mum. But, my big boy, those dimples come from your daddy. I hope he sees you soon. God, Buck doesn't have any idea he fathered a child.

"Mary, I feel so tired. Can you please tuck Pip into bed for me? My strength takes its good old time coming back."

"You have to eat more, Luv," scolded Mary, "You only had a wee bit of toast and a few sips of milk. Did you even take the cod-liver oil, child?"

"Yuk, Of course I did, but it makes me nauseous."

"Well...put it in your orange juice, mind you, it doesn't taste so bad."

"Thanks Mary - surrogate mum and rescuer, you know how much I care, don't you?"

"Of course I do, and you're our daughter, all the family we got."

"Mary, when things turned for the worst, I wrote a letter." Reaching into her pocket, she offered, "I want you to keep this envelope in case anything happens to me."

"Nonsense, Luv."

"No, you must have it to protect little Pip, just in case. I have some money put away so he can have a future. I feel thankful knowing you love him and can take care of him," she added, choking away her tears.

Having settled Pip's future, she fell into a peaceful sleep. Whatever Ilona's future might bring, at least she will not face it alone.

Chapter 26

Surviving

On a blustery day, standing in line at the local grocery store with ration book in hand and baby Pip in his pram, Ilona started to feel like a typical British mother. A woman who detested her dreary life in the city with eternal queuing, cooking, keeping house and watching children.

She wondered how many matriarchs also worked in factories, keeping up the home front for England. Ilona expected her turn to come soon enough. With her cabaret job no longer available, she needed money, not only to survive during this bleak period but to save for her son's future. Even Mary, in her old age, worked as an industrial laborer.

"But if I work, how can I ever leave you, my little darling?" she cooed, nuzzling the cherubic face of tiny Pip against her own, "I'm living this house frau existence without a speck of know-how."

After picking up her rations plus a small, skinned and

dressed rabbit she returned to her flat and heated the range to 350 degrees. Living for weeks on limited provisions, she yearned for some fresh meat. Ilona opened her cabinets, looking for any left-over herbs or spices from long-ago meals. She grumbled when her inventory yielded only salt and pepper.

Sliding her bland hare-onto the oven rack - she squatted on a kitchen chair and reflected, "In Hungary, we ate tasty rabbit when my family stayed on the shore of Balaton. I remember mother preparing it with her aromatic sour cream dressing, parsley potatoes and cabbage soup all infused with paprika. How I miss her delicious food, soothing voice and...and...her."

The new mother fed and settled baby Pip in his crib while waiting for Mary, who always detoured to her flat by the end of a shift at one of the Army's munitions factory.

After a frank conversation about her financial situation, she convinced Mary to rent her the back room again in their Islington flat. This way, Ilona saved the high rent tariff she paid for her West End flat and instead compensated Mary and Mike for rent and child care.

Later, with Mike's approval, she planned to take Mary's place at the plant. Also, little Pip benefited by having a full time baby sitter which delighted Ilona's adopted mother.

Mary quipped, "For the first time, it feels like getting paid to have fun."

*****

For the first several days, Mary arranged to stay and train her how to load .50 caliber rounds for heavy machine guns. Ilona grew familiar with casings, primers, bullets, black powder and metal link belts.

Soon after, she visited a second hand shop and bought some industrial grade pants, shirts and boots. Nothing in her current wardrobe suited the abusive work she now embraced.

With reluctance, Ilona adapted to her new lifestyle of painful calluses and always feeling tired from long hours.

One evening, after working a ten hour shift, Ilona walked her usual fourteen blocks from the industrial area of the city back to the comfort of her room and Pip. However, this night, her stroll turned crude and vulgar.

"Hey Blondie, how about a drink?" offered an inebriated American GI, propping himself up against a filthy brick wall.

"Why the hurry doll face? I have Spam, chocolates, even nylons. Aw, c'mon baby, don't turn your back on a homesick GI. Don't cha want sweet little me under your Christmas tree?"

Ilona ignored the pathetic GI and stepped up her pace. "No wonder I've abandoned any Christmas spirit this year, London smells of bombs, death and the dark side of our Allied soldiers.

"My son and the memories of Buck from last Christmas keep

me going. But, God...I feel so tired, when will I see him again?"

As Mary and Mike's flat came into view, Ilona felt relieved and safe. Even though she escaped Nazi occupation, her unsavory encounter on this night drove home a reality - danger hid in the folds of her world, "ready to pounce without warning."

*****

The dreadful war churned on while Ilona worked ten-hour days, allowing her to make the maximum wage. Topping off her job benefits, this large factory provided a canteen which included one free serving of two vegetables plus meat. A welcome break, it gave Ilona down-time to get off her feet and consume a hot meal.

However, the unpleasant but necessary factory conditions took their toll - deafening machinery noises, disturbed the singer's sensitive ears. When she worked the evening shift and a blackout occurred, all doors and window had to be closed. The trapped dust circulated throughout the factory, irritating Ilona's delicate throat and vocal chords.

Even in daytime, the windows provided no sunlight due to the lattice tape covering them. It prevented splintering glass if the bombs struck too close.

"I swear, this will not last," Ilona declared, "after the war, I can join a cabaret and sing again. But if Buck returns to me, I'll feel grateful just to be his wife and Pip's mum.

"Tomorrow I have the day off and plan to give Mary a break from queuing. I'll use the time to visit Smithville Market and explore the fresh produce.

"Let's see, if I ride the tube for two stops and get off at Moorgate, the walk will take about 10 minutes to the market. Easy enough. Rumor has it; they brought in a supply of rabbits so I'll make rabbit stew for all of us. This time with lots of spices.

"Also, my last trip to the geography section of an open library paid off, it helped me remember Buck's home town. With the war and so much of my life unresolved, I thought it best to write a letter for Buck's parents. Mike and Mary can hold onto it, just in case. I also gave them Karl and Anna's address in Zurich."

*****

"Say it, come on...mum...mum," Mary coaxed Pip.

"Mum, mum, mum," little Pip replied, laughing as he parroted her sounds.

"See there, he can talk," Mary bragged to Mike, "Smart little bloke."

"Hush, Luv!" Mike yelled, "I can't hear the wireless."

He leaned over with his ear next to the speaker. Several minutes later, Mike asked, "Where did Ilona go today?"

"Have ya forgot already? Smithfield Market, Luv, just like she told ya yesterday."

Mike shouted, "One of them bloody V1's hit the market this morning! So far, they counted at least a hundred people dead!"

She grabbed his hand and reasoned, "Let's not panic, ya know how long those food lines can be. Most times, those bombs don't wipe out more than a block anyway."

"Why did she go there in the first place?" anger permeated his question.

"A generous supply of rabbits. Ilona wanted to surprise us by making Hungarian rabbit stew."

Stifling their anxiety, the couple walked fast as possible to Smith Field Market since the tube had been shut down.

Their first vision of devastation took place on one street bordering a corner of the market. Heaps of jagged debris lay strewn about and once familiar buildings - gone. Bobbies, ambulance attendants and other gawkers scurried about trying to make sense of it all.

They roamed about the chaos until a bobby directed them to the staging area for casualties. Numb, somber and in denial, they walked among the rows of dead, staring at the unfamiliar faces.

Passing each one, they hoped she survived - to hear her sweet voice call out – "Mary, Mike, over here." On the last row, with an Army blanket pulled up to her neck, Ilona stared at the sky. Her blond hair, wind-blown and the once perfect face pale and flecked with tiny welts from the blast.

Mary looked at Ilona for a moment in disbelief and then fell to her knees, screaming a chilling sound, almost not human. A primal wail from somewhere deep inside, buried in the fiber of her soul.

She clutched Ilona into her arms and held tight. As Mike pulled away the blanket, he found Ilona's coat saturated with blood. She rocked back and forth, sobbing and muttering, "No...no...wake up, please."

While the authorities went about their business, time stood still for this elderly couple. After losing their son, they had been given a second chance, to love Ilona as their own. Now, the bloody Nazi buzz bombs took her.

A caring witness shared his observations of the scene since he had been working about two blocks from the blast. Running into the square, he first noticed remains destroyed beyond recognition. Outside the block, bodies had been tossed about with great force. He remembered checking Ilona for a pulse but confirmed she died straight away.

Mary and Mike put aside their grief long enough to identify her body for the police. But their loyalty to Ilona went far beyond life or death. Mary refused to let the mortuary truck take her body.

"I won't permit Ilona's body to lie on a table somewhere in the city morgue - God forgive me - waiting to be buried with strangers. I want her to rest next to our son in Hampstead, where you and I will join them someday."

Wiping tears from her cheeks, she directed, "Mike, go fetch

Neville's truck and be quick about it."

*****

"You did her proud, Mary. She looked so beautiful with the way you styled her hair, and our embalmer performed a miracle, fixing the damage on her face.

"When they placed Ilona in our family plot, I thought about all she overcame in her short time. She had raw courage - outfoxed the Nazis in Europe, found a passion with cabaret singing and created a handsome legacy - Pip. Well, Luv...Ilona gave life a good run, her absolute best, she...she can rest easy now."

Patting his hand, she offered, "I know, Luv. Let's finish going through her things. We'll box up the important stuff - for little Pip and Buck too, God willing.

"I remember making this green gown for her when she sang at the cabaret," sobbed Mary, "I just can't believe we'll never see her again. And poor little Pip has no mum now, just us."

"Luv, he has a father somewhere - maybe missing in action or a prisoner of war. Just maybe, he'll come back and take Pip to the states."

"Mike, I though Buck and Ilona made a beautiful couple. Without a doubt, they loved each other. I want him to return from the war - alive - and claim his son but not now.

"We've raised Pip since his birth. Uprooting him before he can understand what happened, will devastate the baby."

"Luv, have ya gone daft? Say what ya mean."

"We must leave the city and find a place near Hampstead. We'll be safer and close to Ilona plus our family too. You and I have enough money to live until we find work."

"I don't agree. Buck has every right to decide Pip's future."

"Look, I know Ilona didn't plan for this to be so complicated. Buck doesn't know he has a son. Also, we haven't the foggiest if he keeps a girlfriend back home."

"Luv, even if we raise Pip until he reaches five or six or even seven, what about Ilona's letter?"

"When we know Buck survived the war and Pip understands he has a father, it will be mailed."

"I hope we don't live to regret manipulating their lives."

"My heart says to give this child good memories, growing up near his mother's grave, getting to know her life. As for Buck, we'll do right by him, when the time comes."

Chapter 27

Death March

The ranking sergeant stepped into Buck's hut and announced, "All right. Listen up men."

All heads turned for his unexpected appearance, "Yeah, yeah, what now, Kelly?" Brooklyn responded.

"The wireless reported a forced march across Germany any day now. The Russians advanced into Lithuania from the east, two days ago, so our Nazi landlords want us out of here.

"Prepare as best you can. Take only what you can carry, this means food and items to trade - you never know. We won't have much time when this happens, so be ready."

None of us ever planned on a winter stroll so we bribed the guards for information on what the commandant had in store. "Perhaps he wanted to use us as bargaining chips for a favorable surrender."

For over a month, I watched flashes of artillery fire in the distance, a good sign of the Allies advancing. Our freedom felt assured but only if we stayed put.

"Just look at us - filthy, starving, sick with dysentery and pneumonia. How the hell do they expect this stalag to go anywhere?" I griped.

One of the kriegies, who used to work in his father's tailor shop, gave us a few easy sewing lessons. We used our shirts, sewed the bottoms together, and with a few other alterations, constructed a handy knapsack.

Each airman tied the sleeves around their shoulders and filled it with personal possessions, leaving hands free. "We can salvage tinned foods from Red Cross parcels if the goons don't puncture them and cigarettes might be good for trading. I have a tooth brush, no tooth paste, but at least I can brush.

"I don't know how long our food will last, but a couple of empty Klim (dried milk product-milk spelled backwards) cans might come in handy for food containers. Some of the guys punched a hole near the top and threaded wire so they attached to their pants. These will be handy for food containers and not take up space in our knapsacks."

"Say Benny, The goons have been talking about the forecast for this winter. They expect it to be one of the coldest on record.

"If the commandant wants us to traipse around the countryside, we need thicker coats and pants. Hah, we both know he has no conscience. He'll just let us freeze to death out on the road."

"Geeze Buck, stop being so pessimistic. Now you've got me thinking about my sheepskin lined bomber jacket. The damn Jerry's grabbed it along with my watch, right after they captured me. The bastards consider them trophies."

"Yeah, for me, I need my warm boots. I just hope this march won't last too long. One of the goons told me they loaded our sickest men on a train, early this morning. Lucky bastards, they don't have to wade through this deep snow."

On February sixth, the Waffen-SS gave us less than an hour to gather our Spartan belongings and prepare to march.

Kelly roused every able airman from the huts and led them to the assembly area. He barked, "Line up men, single file. Each airman in turn, will proceed to the stack of Red Cross parcels. Take anything you want but only if you can carry it."

Buck interrupted, "Wow, Sergeant, where the hell did they hide all those boxes?"

"They never said or apologized - the bastards. I recommend taking K-ration meals, candy bars and maybe cigarettes or soap to trade."

An aura of unrestrained happiness prevailed over the men as they loaded up. But in their frail condition, I feared the provisions might prove too heavy for some.

I watched with curiosity as they divided us into groups of about 300 and headed in different directions. Scuttlebutt from the goons said our bombs may have torn up some of the roads. To the naive, spreading out might make sense, but I didn't believe them.

"Hey Buck, the guards assigned me to a group behind you. With this cold and snow, do you think we'll be all right?"

"Don't worry Benny, everything will work out fine. Just...stay in the middle of your group, no eye contact with the goons and most important - pace your K-rations. Hey, we'll see each other real soon."

"Sure, sure, thanks for the good advice, Buck."

Poor Benny, although no one else noticed, I saw the hint of fear in his eyes. Sometimes I forget he hasn't even reached eighteen yet.

"Yo Brooklyn, looks like you made this elite group."

"Only the best, Buck, only the best."

One of the guards, dressed in a thick wool coat and heavy boots pushed toward us and yelled, "Alle, bewegen jetzt." Only a few of us understood he wanted our group to move - now. Looking around me, I told everyone to start walking.

So...without any trumpets or fanfare, our dismal group marched, wading through snow above our ankles and shivering non-stop from the bone chilling weather. Soon enough, we realized this trek pushed our feeble endurance beyond the limits of exhaustion.

During short rest stops, we started to abandon some of our provisions, keeping just the K-ration meals and a few packs of cigarettes. Some of the stronger men kept soap since the goons liked to bargain food for an aromatic bar of Ivory.

On the first night we took refuge in a barn. We found the horse shelter lacking in space, so our group slept on the dirt floor by leaning against each other.

We soon realized they lied about our short walk. Some days, we marched at least fifteen miles. When they started a routine pattern of zigging and zagging, it grew evident they wanted to avoid a confrontation with the Russians.

Our Red Cross provisions ran out after several weeks and without any food or medical attention from our captors, survival of the fittest, ruled every day. Weak and starving, we tried to help those who fell behind but when a man's body succumbed to dysentery or pneumonia, he grew too fragile to walk.

Brooklyn and I started to carry an airman nicknamed Slugger because he loved the St. Louis Cardinals. Even though the wind bit our exposed skin, we knew he had a raging fever. Almost incoherent, he rambled on about his wife and new baby.

"Buck...Buck, you have kids?"

"Nah, no wife or kids yet, Slugger."

"Yeah? Well...I never thought much of babies either until my wife gave me little Joey. He looks just like me. Hey, I'll teach him to play ball when he grows up.

"Aah. Guys - I feel so bad. Have we reached Missouri yet? I just want to crawl into my bed and sleep for a week."

I looked at Brooklyn and shook my head. We knew he needed a doctor and penicillin but those filthy Nazi bastards didn't lift a finger to help him.

We carried him for two more days, but at sunset, Brooklyn and I noticed, Slugger didn't respond to us. When the goons found out, they made us move him to the rear of the group.

As our team walked on, these dregs of the Third Reich made us carry Slugger to a side of the road.

"Setzte ihn ab" (put him down), they yelled as one pointed a gloved finger to the snow covered ground. I looked at my own bare hands and refused to move. If Brooklyn's rage filled face had the capacity to kill, I imagined both of those goons laying face down in the road.

After several minutes of cursing us, the SS filth raised their rifles and aimed at our heads. In crude English, the senior guard said, "Last time, put him down."

I knew they had no conscience about shooting us since I had seen it before. Shooting of airmen for any arbitrary reason came sanctioned by the commandant. The goons didn't have the mentality or authority to commit war crimes on their own.

We lowered him into several inches of snow, buttoned the collar and straightened his arms at the side, like at attention but lying down. Although Slugger seemed to breathe he never stirred leading me to think he entered a comatose state.

The younger goon walked us back to the group while the other stayed behind, minutes later a single shot rang out. In my weakened condition, I felt helpless but incensed to the marrow. Inside the deepest recesses of my mind, I screamed, "Damn you, damn you all to hell!"

When I calmed down, one thought consumed me; Slugger might have survived if we stayed at the camp. "His death, and for the rest of us who don't make it - our deaths will fall on the shoulders of this commandant. I believe there will be a day of reckoning for him."

As our march continued, we encountered POWs from other camps and exchanged news about our experiences, however, the guards kept us moving. As nightfall approached, we sought shelter in barns, if not, we slept outside, huddling together just to stay warm. Our survival relied on a diet of meager slices of black bread and boiled potatoes.

One foggy evening, after marching through a farming area, the team settled into an abandoned machine shed. Most of the group collapsed where they stood. However, I pulled off my shoes and socks to check for blisters and frost bite.

As I started to put them back on, Brooklyn entered the shed. I hadn't even noticed how or when he left.

"What the hell? Where did you just come from? Why haven't the goons roughed you up for leaving the shed?"

"Those SS bastards took up residence in the farm house. They left one outside but he seems too interested in building a bonfire. Besides, with this fog, you can't see but a few feet."

Brooklyn smiled for the first time in weeks and then looked down at the bulge in his coat. He whispered, "A chicken, Buck, I got us a chicken."

Leaving on all fours, we crawled behind the shed and like madmen, plucked the feathers, ripped it in half and ate everything. I felt the half chicken sit heavy in my stomach, but for the first time took comfort in the thought - I can survive this.

Through our arduous travels, some farmers took pity and gave us a bowl of soup or boiled potatoes and in one case, slaughtered a cow. In spite of these good Samaritans, airmen still died from pneumonia and exposure.

In desperation, the Germans gave us liberty to scrounge our own meals. On a good day, we found unclaimed crops in the fields or potatoes from a farmer's larder. During the worst of times, we roasted cats or dogs over an open fire.

As winter turned to spring, the snow which provided water to quench our thirst began to disappear. We drank contaminated water from creeks and puddles along-side the road. As a result, many of us suffered from diarrhea, fever and abdominal pain. Those who lost the most weight and lacked a strong will to survive - died.

We all developed a buddy system to monitor each other's intake of food and bolster spirits. Our goal - survival at any cost since we knew the Allies battled just miles away. Brooklyn and I struggled every day just to get up push through the day.

The pace of those still alive slowed to a shuffle and the guards seemed demoralized. Brooklyn overheard some goons discussing their options if captured by the Russians. They feared ending up in the notorious Vorkuta Gulag.

On a gloomy spring day while walking through mild rain, Brooklyn stopped for a moment and lamented, "Buck, I've been putting this off for some time now. I'll just sit on the bank right here and make my peace. The guards will do the rest. You've been a good friend but I just can't make it another day."

"What the hell? Don't you dare quit on me. We talked about this - you keep me going and I keep you going - a two man team.

"And the Allies, remember the Allies, look over there at the east horizon. I expect to see them walking through the tree line any hour now. Besides, I need ya kid. Who else can translate what these goons say?"

"God damn it Buck, I ache with constant pain. Look at my ankles, swollen to twice their size. And my feet - blisters the size of quarters."I know, I know, everybody has the same thing so don't complain.

"But I feel like a bull gored me in the stomach. Something

has to be infected inside there. Forget the humiliation of taking a crap where you stand, looking at the blood and pus coming out scares me the most. I can't keep anything down which means I'll starve to death soon."

"Don't give up on me, Brooklyn; several weeks ago, I saved a couple hands full of charcoal embers from the cooking fires. One of the old guys said it helped ease his symptoms. Now chew on them and consider it an order."

*****

By my reckoning, we had marched, foraged for food, bivouacked in some vile places and watched our buddies die for about three months, give or take. The sound of shelling grew so close, I almost smelled gunpowder in the air.

SS Wehrmacht guards started to act with civility, realizing their time had almost run its course. Some of them even shared their tins of sardines.

With the anticipated turn of events, a few, in their weak state of mind, felt sufficient euphoria to think about escaping. We talked our fellow airmen out of it - freedom approached in days. Why risk a bullet in the back?

Birds chirped overhead against a blue sky and warm breezes from the Baltic embraced our rag-tag group as the goons moved us through North Germany toward Lübeck.

One foot in front of the other, scanning the horizon, wondering when our liberators will pounce on these soon-to-be POWs. Those thoughts churned over and over in my mind - waiting - waiting.

Just outside Rostock, on a flat stretch of dirt road lined with forest, at least a hundred British soldiers emerged from the tree line. They held - model 303 rifles - tight against their shoulders, each aimed at the SS Waffen guards.

The Nazis laid down their rifles in a pile by the wayside and with their hands high in the air, submitted to a search for hidden weapons, papers and anything else crucial to understanding the Third Reich's intentions. Then, one by one, the Brits rounded them up like cattle and sat them down with hands behind their heads.

If our group, resembling skeletons, had the energy, I think we might have jumped up and down, screaming until our voices went hoarse. Instead, we just stood there, stoop shouldered - some crying, others silent with disbelief and a few even smiling, but above all, grateful our nightmare had come to an end.

The British commander told us they had been marching from the west, liberating camps in North Germany when they came upon our group. They also expected to meet up with the Russians soon, coming from the east.

I remembered, when based outside London, we called these good lads - Tommys. They distributed food rations and water to everyone and a field intelligence office interviewed each one of us. Before the captain finished with me, he offered, "Welcome back to the Allied effort. Remember this date, May 3, 1945, on your first step back to freedom."

Those of our group too sick for travel stayed with the medic. As for the rest, our English Allies kept us together until they arranged for transportation. I guess they feared we might ravage the nearby farms and their women. Although we all struggled with the thought of revenge, our lack of vigor prevented us from doing either.

As we boarded one of their olive drab camouflage trucks, I consoled, "Hey Brooklyn, we made it, see kid, I told ya."

Nodding his head, he responded, "Thanks Buck, with your help and prodding, I made it."

Our truck bounced over country roads for several hours until we arrived at a large compound with old world, stone architecture and high peaked roof. Our driver told us it used to be a German officer's training facility.

Once inside, a corporal showed our team to the processing area. We showered, shaved and tolerated a delousing. After this intensive treatment, our guide walked us to the supply room for a uniform fitting, followed by hair cut and hot meal.

Next, we reported to their health facility for an assessment of each airman's medical condition. The doc said my blood pressure topped out over 140 on the high end and I had a viral infection putting my temperature near 100 degrees.

We had been recuperating in sickbay for several days when a captain visited. He informed us of Russian reports about Hitler's death. He also spoke the words which all of us wanted to hear, "We won the war. The BBC says Germany will sign an unconditional surrender on May 7th in Reims, France."

Because the Tommys liberated, fed and clothed our team, we came under their jurisdiction and had to abide by British Army rules. After we had a chance to build up our strength, they planned to transport half of us further west to Camp Lucky Strike in France for additional processing.

The Tommys also arranged to transport the other half to a facility near Oxford, England. Because of the high influx of liberated POW's, resources in France soon exhausted. After volunteering for Oxford, I secured a seat on the next plane bound for England.

Upon our arrival, we submitted to additional delousing in a dedicated hangar to insure no foreign organisms found their way into the general population.

Afterward, their base cafeteria served a light snack as we prepared for the final briefing. My senior intelligence officer asked penetrating questions and listened with full attention as I recounted endless horrific stories of life in captivity.

When the processing finished, they bussed us to a military hospital where we stayed for two weeks. During this stay, besides getting medical attention, we ate anything we chose. However, the doc cautioned moderation, given our compromised digestive system.

I soon felt strong enough to travel; however, the commander announced flights to the states backed up and to expect delays for several weeks.

With my heart racing, I seized an opportunity to ask the officer in charge, "Sir, I want to apply for a three-day pass to London."

"So...Staff Sergeant Remke, you do understand, most of the city lies in ruin? What motivates a young man like you to go there?"

"Sir, I need to find someone. A person very important to me. We have unfinished business which I've neglected much too long."

"Well...without a doubt, you've earned some time off. I think we can work it out."

"Thank you sir, I appreciate it."

Chapter 28

Return to London

As I walked to the bus stop, a voice called out, "Sergeant, I overheard your conversation. Headed to London, then?"

"Yes Lieutenant, on the West End."

"Hop in Sergeant, I happen to be going near the same area. My mum lives in Kensington. Wetmore, Hank Wetmore here. And who might you be?"

“Walter Remke, but you can call me Buck."

"Well...Buck. When did you last visit the Big Smoke?"

"Geez, seems like a lifetime ago. But, I guess about this time, last year.

"Sir, I notice you've been awarded a number of medals for serving England. I feel quite honored to be hitching a ride with an RAF Flight Lieutenant."

"Thanks. Yes...I've earned a few. The top one - Distinguished Flying Medal in '42 and the next - Distinguished Flying Cross in '44 for our mission over Holland. Command assigned me to some of the most critical missions of the war. However, I doubt if there will be any medal for my time held captive by the Nazis.

"But enough about me, Sergeant? What sends you to London?"

"I need to find a woman...Ilona László, sir. We had grown rather close in '43 and '44...up until my mission over Normandy."

"I see, Sergeant. Tell me, how did you meet Ilona?"

"Well, sir, I met her in a cabaret on the West End. The joint features her as the headline singer for the evening show."

"A cabaret singer, by Jove? How exciting."

"Yes sir. But not your home grown, average cabaret singer. An upper class Hungarian, she studied classical music in the Music Academy in Budapest. As for looks, she stands out in any crowd."

"How much do you know about her? What about her family?"

"She has no family, mother and father died in Budapest. After the Nazis occupied Hungary, they lost their business. Ilona believes the stress of anti-Semitism and war, over time, killed them. Her uncle, who financed her trip to London, passed away about two years ago.

"The Hungarian Second Army reported her only brother, as killed-in-action somewhere in Russia."

"Poor bloke."

"Yeah, but in spite of losing everyone and avoiding the Gestapo, she managed to flee East Europe by risking a dangerous trek across several Nazi occupied countries."

"Bravo for her. If I may ask, unless she picked up English as a child, the change in language must have been difficult."

"Ilona told me she studied with a first-class tutor outside London, until her uncle died of a heart attack. Afterward, she picked it up from Londoners, first working with dishwashers in a cabaret and then from an elderly couple in Islington."

"Well...your woman sounds like an ace, the bees knees."

"Yeah, she never settles for less and knows her own mind. With the help of her friends and perseverance, she auditioned at the Black Cat and won a full time singing gig."

"You say...the Black Cat Cabaret? My flying associates and I used to go there until the bloody Doodlebugs flattened it."

"Sir?"

"Sorry old Chap, I can see you've been caught unaware. I didn't mean to act so beastly."

"Oh my God," I exclaimed, trying to fight back negative

images of Ilona during an evening show. In mid-song, her essence splintering into a million pieces of flesh and bone. I looked out the side window, avoiding Hank's sad face, trying to hold back a rising tide.

"Do you know if anyone died in the explosion?"

"Yes, I remember reading it in the newspaper. They pulled at least thirty people out of the rubble. I don't recall any details though.

"Buck, you can't jump to any conclusions, wait until you contact the authorities."

Hank appeared quite logical but I still fought back tears for what might be. Without my permission, a warm, wet stream found its way down my cheek.

While I feared for Ilona, without warning, all the atrocities of last year flashed through my mind. Every brutality and deprivation pent up inside came spilling out.

"Get it out, Buck. You've been through bloody hell and back."

Gaining my composure, I reflected. "Sorry...not your fault Hank. I had this notion of walking into the cabaret and picking up where we left off. It...it seems I also brought some baggage back from Germany.

"Ilona - I have to focus on her. Maybe she took the night off or escaped."

"I have an idea, Buck, rather than dropping you off at a

canteen, join me while I visit my mum. You'll love her. Afterward, we can embark on a quest around London to find your singer."

"I didn't intend to take up your time like this, but thanks for your help."

*****

As we motored through bombed out city streets, many of the landmarks I remembered on Essex and Liverpool Road, no longer existed. Many streets no longer served as thoroughfares - impassable. So often, we turned around and tried another road.

Hank lamented, "The BBC said Hitler vented his rage for the Allied invasion of Normandy by raining down those Doodlebugs on London.

"Before we left the Oxford Processing Center this morning, I chatted with some officers about the technical aspects of the Nazi V1s (aka buzz bombs, doodlebugs).

"The buggers fly without a pilot, at a range of just under 93 kilometers. They can be launched from almost anywhere along the French or Holland Coast. With an air-speed of about 248 kilometers per hour, they reach London in 25 minutes.

"While you struggled to survive in a POW camp, those blooming Nazis fired off 50 to 100 a day in late June of '44."

"Hank, we've been traveling all afternoon. Every property

looks gutted, a blackened shell or no building at all, just a pile of rubble. I don't pretend to comprehend the total loss of life incurred but it must have been in the tens of thousands."

"It breaks my heart to know such large numbers of fellow Londoners died, Buck. Although the V1s killed thousands, the V2s leveled whole blocks.

"With the help of our agents in Germany, we discovered they carried a one ton warhead and Nazi scientists designed them as long range rockets. The Jerrys fired from mobile launchers in Germany and occupied Low Countries.

"London had no counter-measure to stop them. By the time we picked them up on radar screens, our pilots had just five minutes to respond."

"Good God, how did your mother fair in all of this destruction?"

"Mum, like most Londoners, managed to survive in underground stations. Part of her neighborhood in Kensington took a hit. However, Mum had the good fortune of living in North Kensington."

"Buck, at this rate we won't make Islington until nightfall. I know a small hotel in Pimlico on the West End near Victoria Station. They don't charge much and welcome servicemen. Like most, it has facilities down the hall, but they keep it clean. Why don't I drop you off there and we can continue this adventure tomorrow morning?"

"Thank you. Although we just met today, you've been such a

good friend. I appreciate everything you've done for me, Hank."

"This escapade has been good for me too, Buck. I can't sit around thinking about my time as a POW. Too much idle time drives me crazy."

Entering the small two story hotel, I checked in with the elderly lady at the front desk. A few civilians and soldiers sat in the lobby, reading or chatting with each other.

Floral patterns dominated walls of the hallway and bright lights provided guidance to my room. It seemed small but spotless. Much different than Hitler's hotel where I spent the last year of my life. Ah, heaven, just to sleep in a bed with clean sheets.

I didn't mind using the common facilities. I caught up on reading a guide to getting around London, provided by the center. Around midnight, most of the guest activity had subsided. I used the time to soak in a hot bath without interruption. It reminded me of my last Christmas with Ilona.

While relaxing in the tub, an array of questions ran through my head, "Ilona, did they pull your dead body out of the cabaret? Does it explain why you haven't answered my letters?

"If I can just remember the names of her friends. That Christmas they invited us over for dinner. Come on, think. Mike...and...and...Mary, okay, but I never caught their last names. Damn. For sure, I know they lived in Islington."

My hotel fare included breakfast in a small, but busy dining room. Though they rationed the food, and my appetite still remained poor, I tolerated some hot porridge and enjoyed their royal treatment.

"Some more coffee, Yank? And how about a refill on the porridge?"

"Thanks, it sits easy in my stomach. I have a hard time keeping food down after starving for the past year."

"Sounds like the bloody bastards took you to Sausage Hill."

"Sir?"

"You know - Sausage Hill, taken prisoner by the Germans."

"Oh yeah, they sure did."

"Glad you're back and getting on with your life. What brings you to London?"

"Looking for a special lady, last saw her in May of '44. She sang at the Black Cat Cabaret and lived on the West End, near the Covent Garden area."

"Going to be hard, sergeant, the bloody Doodlebugs took a mean chunk out of the place. Hope you find her.

"Well...be right back with the coffee and porridge."

He leaned over my table and shared, "We appreciate you lads fighting along-side our boys. We'll never forget it."

I finished my meal, packed the few personal items and

waited outside for Hank. Several minutes later he pulled up in his jeep.

I enjoyed his company as well as the generosity of this gentleman. He characterized my idea of a proper RAF officer; uniform pressed, shoes spit-shined, maybe with his mum's help.

However, because of his life in a camp, he seemed much older than his thirty years. I wonder what my family will say when they see me.

"Hank, sure you don't mind driving me around the Big Smoke?"

"Buck, old man, my pleasure. Good to have a break from my mum fussing and feeding me, I've been kissed by enough elderly relatives to last me a lifetime.

"Don't misunderstand, I appreciate their attention, given they thought I died when my plane crashed. Even after Mum received a wire announcing my prisoner of war status, she believed the Nazis shot all RAF pilots."

"Where did they take you after being interrogated?"

"The SS incarcerated me at Stalag Luft III. Did you hear about the fifty British officers, executed after escaping from there? The bloody Nazis had no right.

"At one time Germany agreed to honor all rules of the Geneva Convention, but Hitler ignored them to make an example out of our lads. Those damn Jerrys knew the Allied officer's first duty must be to escape, yet killed them in cold blood. I hope the inevitable war crime trials will give the SS a taste of their own medicine."

"Hank, it seems entrenched in every conversation I've had with other airmen. I think this atrocity will stain Germany forever."

"Well...let's not dwell on those horrors any more. Today, we have a mission to find this special woman in your life."

"Where do you want to go first?"

"We'll drive around a bit and investigate what remains of the Black Cat. Don't get your hopes up, but my mum read the newspaper article about the hit. She doesn't recall seeing Ilona László listed as a casualty."

As we drove further into the city, I inquired, "How come those women stand in line outside the food store?"

"By Jove, you've been out of touch. They call it queuing. The government rations our food just like America. You see, when they run out, they either do without or go to the black market."

After negotiating the destruction spread of rubble throughout the city, Hank drove to Islington. "Odd, how different it looks after the bombings. The mass of fallen buildings slumped in scattered piles.

"Wow, Pop criticized poor construction on any building but these fell way below his standards. He always insists on a strong concrete foundation and solid wood beams to support the brickwork.

"These structures must have been slapped together and as a result, crumbled with little resistance. Of course, I imagine, not even well built structures survived a direct hit."

"Buck, does anything look familiar to you? The neighborhood or street?"

"Yeah, go in this direction, past those row houses. I remember Ilona taking me down a narrow street to the elderly couple's flat. Wait...right there. The red brick building on the second floor."

"You lucked out, Yank, in spite of all of the rubble, most of this block remains intact. Let's knock on the door and see what we can find out."

"Damn it, Hank, the flat looks empty. I hoped to find them still here, just wishful thinking. My time just ran out. By this afternoon, I must get back to the center and take care of any paperwork and packing. I ship out state-side, the next morning."

"Don't give up quite yet. How about the flat next door? Look at the old woman gawping into the hallway through her open door. Maybe she knows where they moved."

I approached the elderly lady and initiated, "Good morning, ma'am, Sergeant Remke here and my associate Lieutenant Wetmore.

"I see no one lives in the flat next door. During the winter of '44, my girlfriend, Ilona László, and I celebrated Christmas here, with Mike and Mary. Do you know where they moved?"

She questioned, "Be ya Buck Remke from the states?"

"Yes, everyone calls me by my nickname, Buck. I hail from Pennsylvania."

"Well...the old couple moved several months ago. Didn't leave a new address. They left an envelope for you though. Wait here, I'll get it for you."

When she returned, the elderly woman carried it in both hands. Odd, I had an eerie feeling, like the envelope had religious significance.

A bit surprised, I accepted the packet and started to open it.

She put her hand over mine and offered, "Please come inside and have a seat, Buck."

Sitting on the edge of her couch, nervous, I folded up the flap and pulled out a white envelope. I started to read the hand written letter.

*****

Dear Buck,

It breaks my heart to tell you, a V2 killed our sweet Ilona on March 8, 1945 at the Smithfield Market.

Her death left us with deep grief and many unresolved

issues. When our pain has diminished, we will share the last moments of her life.

In addition to the danger of V2s, the Islington area no longer has any meaning for us so we left the city.

Please know she received a beautiful and respectful burial.

Love,

Mary

*****

"No, No, No. Please God. No," I turned numb with denial. Ilona gone...forever? On top of this, flashes of all the pain and torture I suffered in Germany brought me to my knees.

Hank thanked the woman for bringing me closure. The sad look on her face told me, she also felt the pain of my loss.

In the hallway, Hank suggested, "Let's get out of here, I think about now, a pint or two will do you good."

"Yeah, you bet, I just can't deal with this, right now. I never had a chance to say good-bye."

I don't remember much of the afternoon or ride back to the center. Downing some coffee, I filled out my transfer papers, mouthed the words, "Yes Sir, Yes Sir." Like a robot, I hobbled onto the troop ship in Northampton, landed a bottom bunk and slept most of the way, until reaching dock-side in New York Harbor.

*****

"Buck, Buck," echoed from the pier as I saw mom waving little Victor's hand and pop smiling, though he never smiled. My two crazy brothers, Miles and Paul ran up the ship's ramp until the MPs caught them.

After hugs and kisses, we packed into the old Chevy. On the drive home, everyone asked a million questions - about me and the war, except for Pop. I watched, as he sat behind the wheel, driving in quiet strength, his strong jaw set with an aura of satisfaction.

Of course, home never looked so good. Our garden - bigger than when I left and they called it a Victory Garden. Since most of the neighbors had small farms, they inundated us with fried chicken, eggs, home-made cakes and pies.

They created a flurry of well meaning activity - welcoming me back. I apologized for not being too conversant, but I guess the year of my life in captivity took away the spirit for small talk and the loss of Ilona fractured my inner soul.

*****

Seven years after the 8th Army Air Force discharged me, I still struggled to get my life back in order. Pop told me to snap out of it. Mom insisted on feeding me and trying to hug my year of torture away. While many of my high school buddies moved on, married, had children, I lived with Mom, Pop and my brothers.

I turned to alcohol for relief, but it didn't solve the recurrent nightmares or take away my fear of loud noises and claustrophobia. Since I suffered from an intangible wound inside my head, the Veteran's Administration seemed incapable of helping me.

With assistance from the GI Bill, I enrolled into an apprentice program for bricklayers. I decided to dedicate my life to carry on Pop's legacy as a creator of beautiful homes and buildings.

On a warm, Saturday morning, I pulled my Hudson next to the hand pump on our front lawn and started to wash its roof. Mom came out of the house on her usual morning stroll to the mail box.

On her way back, she scurried toward me, a startled look on her face. Out of breath, Mom grabbed my arm and rasped, "Buck, the mailman delivered this letter to you. According to the return address, it came from Ilona László."

END

BIBLIOGRAPHY

Books

Ambrose, Stephen E. D-Day. June 6, 1944. New York: Simon & Schuster, 1995.

Bradely, James. Fly Boys: A True Story of Courage. New York: Little, Brown & Co., 2003.

Brighton, Terry. Patton, Montgomery, Rommel, Masters of War. New York: Crown Publishers, 2008.

Brombert, Victor. Trains of Thought. Memories of a Stateless Youth. New York, London: W.W. Norton, 2002.

Burrin, Philippe. France Under the Germans - Collaboration and Compromise. New York: The New York Press, 1996.

Bussel, Norman. My Private War. New York: Pegasus Books LLC., 2008.

Carroll, I.M. The Great Escape from Stalag Luft III. New York: Pocketbooks, 2004.

Christiansen, Chris. Seven Years Among Prisoners of War. Athen, Ohio: Ohio University Press, 1994.

Countdown to War. The American Story WWII. Alexandria, VA: Time and Life Books, 1997.

Freeman, Roger A. The Mighty Eighth in Color. Stillwater, MN: Specialty Press, 1992.

Groom, Winston. 1942. New York: Grove/Atlantic, Inc., 2005.

Hillenbrand, Lauren. Unbroken. New York: Random House, 2010.

Karsai, László, Gábor Kádár & Zoltán Vági. From Deprivation of Rights to Genocide. (To the Memory of the Hungarian Holocaust). Budapest: Blackprint Nyomda, 2006.

Kee, Robert. A Crowd is Not Company. London: Phoenix Press, 2000.

Kluger, Ruth. Still Alive, A Holocaust Girlhood Remembered. New York: The Feminine Press, 2001.

Miller, Donald. The Story of World War II. New York: Simon & Schuster, 1986.

Murray, W. & A. Millett. A War to be Won: Fighting the Second World War. New York: Bellnat Press, 1950.

Nichols, David & Studs Terkel. Ernie's War. New York: Simon and Schuster, 1986.

Okerstram, Dennis, R. The Final Mission of Bottoms Up. Columbia, MO: University of Missouri Press, 2011.

Richard, Oscar G III. Kriegie. Baton Rouge: Louisiana State University Press, 2000.

Ovey, Richard. Why the Allies Won. New York: W.W. Norton, 1940.

Prange, Gordon. At Dawn We Slept. New York: Penguin Books, 1991.

Reynolds, David. In Command of History. New York: Random House, 2005.

Rice, Earl Jr. The Final Solution. San Diego: The Holocaust Library, Lucent Books, Inc., 1998.

Stafford, David. Ten Days to D-Day. New York: Little, Brown & Co., 2003.

Stargardt, Nicholas. Witnesses of War. New York: Alfred A. Knopf, a Division of Random House, 2005.

Stewart, Sidney. Give Us This Day. New York, London: W.W. Norton, 1957.

The American Story World War II. Alexandria, VA: Time and Life Books, 1997.

Waller, Maureen. London 1945. New York: St. Martin's Griffin, 2004.
Williams, Charles. Pétain. New York: Palgrave, Macmillan, 2005.
Wintraub, Stanley. Eleven Days in December. New York: Free Press. A Division of Simon and Schuster, 1944.

Internet Sites Visited

Arizona Wing of the Commemorative Air Force. (n.d.) *Crew Positions in a B-17 FLYING FORTRESS.* Retrieved from http://azcaf.org/pages/contact.html on 02/14/12.
Auschwitz Concentration Camp. Wikipedia, the free encyclopedia. Retrieved from http://en.wikipedia.org/wki/Auschwitz_concentration_camp on 09/25/2012.
US Air Force History Support Office. (n.d.) *B-17 Flying Fortress.* Retrieved from http://www.battle-fleet.com/pw/his/b17.htm on 08/22/11.
A Brief History of the U.S. Army in World War II. (2003) Published by the U.S. Army Center for Military History. Retrieved from website www.history.army.mil/brocures/reference/fpr.htm on 09/10/11.
Chen, C. Peter. (2004-2012). *B-17 Flying Fortress* Published by World War II Database. Retrieved from http://ww2db.com on 10/31/12.
Dyess, William E. (2009). *The Dyess Story. 1943 The Bataan Death March, 1942.* EyeWitness to History. www.eyewitnesstohistory.com.
Retrieved from http://www.eyewitnessto history.com/pfbataandeathmarch.htmeyewitnesstohistor on 05/15/11.
English-German Dictionary. (2002-2012). Dict.cc. Retrieved from http://www.dict.cc?s=Stehen+bleiben on 02/12/2012.
Hatton, Greg. (July 15, 1944). *American Prisoners of War in German, Stalag Luft 4*:Military Intelligence Service War Department.
Retrieved from http://wwwb24.net/pow/stalag4.htm on 03/07/12.
Hatton, Greg. (August 1989) *The Heydekrug Run.* 1944.
Retrieved from http://www.b24.net/stories/hatton.htm on 03/07/12.
Henden, Stephen. *Flying Bombs and Rockets.* (n.d.)
Retrieved from www.flyingbombsandrockets.com/Timeline.html on 10/07/11.
Holocaust Remembrance and Beyond (2002-2012) Isurvived.org. Holocaust Survivors and Remembrance Project, NatureQuest Publications, Inc.
Retrieved from http://isurvived.org/about.html on 06/19/11.
Home Front 1939-45 - Rationing. (n.d.)
Retrieved from http://www.historyonthenet.com/WW2/home_front.htm on 05/15/11.
Horne, Alstar & Hart Liddell. (2002). *Blitzkrieg, 1940.* Eyewitness to History, www.eyewitnesstohistory.com .
Retrieved from http://www,eyewitnessto history.com/pfblitxkrieg.htm on 05/15/11.
Maps of World War II. Western Front 1944-45 Battle of the Bulge. (n.d.)
Retrieved from http://www.onwar.com/maps/wwii/westfront/bulge4445.htm on 09/01/11.
Oil Campaign Chronology of World War II. (2012). Wikipedia, the free encyclopedia.
Retrived from http://en.wikipedia.org/wiki/Oil_Campaign_chronology_of_World_War_II on 06/01/12.
Rigg, Brian Mark. (2008). *Nuremberg Laws. Encyclopaedia Judaica.* Jewish Virtual Library.

The Gale Group. Retrieved from http://www.jewishvirtuallibrary.org/source/judaica/ejud-002-0015-0-14977.html on 06/19/11.

Ronan, Thomas.(2010). *Bomb Map V1 Flying Bomb strike at Aldwych.* June 30, 1944. Retrieved from http://www.westendatwar.org.uk/page_id_197_path_op28p.aspx on 06/26/11.

Thomas, Ronan. (2010).*The Blitz 1940-1945*. Westminster City Archives. Retrieved from westendatwar.org.uk/index.aspx on 03/05/12.

Sayre,Joel. (2006). *Berlin in Defeat, 1945*. www.eyewitnesstohistory.com. Retrieved from http://www.eyewitnesstohistory.com/berlindefeat.htm on 05/15/11.

World History/Causes and Course of the Second World War. (2012) Wikipedia, the free encyclopedia. Retrieved from website, http://en.wikibooks.org/wiki/World_History/Causes_and_course_of_the_Second_World_War#The_Phony_War_and_Night_in_Scandanavia_.28Winter_1939_April_1940.29 on 04/12/11.

World War 2 Timelines 1939 - 1945. (n.d.) Retrieved from www.worldwar-2.net/index.htm on 10/10/11.

World War Two - German Prisoner of War Camps. (n.d.) Retrieved from http://www.history on the net.com/WW2/german_pow_camps.htm on 03/19/12.

Reconnaissance Patrol, 1943, The Invasion of Sicily. (2007). EyeWitness to History, www.eyewitnesstohistory.com. Retrieved from http://www.eyewitnesstohistory.com/sicily.htm on 05/15/11.

Interviews

Interview with George Taylor, author of the November 05, 1988 "*Times News*" article "One of Many". The story of Nicholas Young, a Tamaqua High School teacher and former POW.

Interview with László Csösz, Historian of the Holocaust Memorial Center. Budapest, HU.

Interview with Miklós Ebner, Museum Guide of the Dohány Street Synagogue. Budapest, HU.

Interview with former POW Nicholas Young, Civics Teacher from Tamaqua, PA.

Interview with former POW Norman Bussell, Author of "My Private War".

Interview with William (Mickey) Arner, a private pilot who detailed more of the antics of Edgar and Stanley Arner's barn-storming days.

Places Traveled For Research

Auschwitz Concentration Camp, Oswiecim, Poland.

District XIII, St. István Park area. Budapest, HU.

Dohány Street Synagogue, Budapest, HU.

Eagle's Nest, Munich, Germany.

Holocaust Museum, Budapest, HU.

House of Terror Museum, Budapest, HU.

Music

Berlin, Irving. *White Christmas.* 1942. New York: Irving Berlin Inc., 1942. Print.

Freeson, Neville & Albert Von Tilzer. *I'll Be There in Apple Blossom Time.* 1920. New York: Broadway Music Corp., 1920. Print.

Gannon, Kim, Walter Kent & Buck Ram. *I'll Be Home for Christmas.* 1943. New York: Melrose Music Corp, 1943. Print.

Parker, Ross & Hughie Charles. *We'll Meet Again.* 1939. London: The Irwin Dash Music Co. Ltd. 1939. New York: Dash Connelly, Inc.

Puccini, Giacomo. (1896). *La Bohéme.* Milan: Casa Ricordi.

Bizet, George. (1875). *Carmen.* Paris: Dover.